The Book of Everything

Books by Maik Nwosu

Novels
Invisible Chapters
Alpha Song
A Gecko's Farewell
The Book of Everything

Poetry
Suns of Kush
Stanzas from the Underground

Short Stories
Return to Algadez

Drama
A Quintet for Dawn

The Book of Everything
by
Maik Nwosu

CROSSROADS
New York, 2025

Published by
CROSSROADS
1178 Broadway
3rd Floor, #1333
New York, NY 10001

© 2025 by Maik Nwosu. All rights reserved.
Printed in the United States of America
Cover art: Victor Ekpuk

This is a work of fiction. All names, characters, places, and incidents are products of the author's imagination or are used fictitiously.

ISBN 979-8-9904712-5-2

Library of Congress Control Number: 2024905054

The Book of Everything

1

I have seen the future, and it is something like the past.

My grandfather came back from the dead forty-four years, four months, and four days after his funeral. It was almost as if he chose the date himself. And, in a sense, he did. It was the last day in the first week of a new academic year. I was scheduled to teach Global Englishes that semester and I had just finished my introductory class. It was not really a class, just an opportunity to talk about the class in the hope that doing so would make a difference. "Hello, my name is Ile, and I came to the US from Nigeria a long time ago..." After I said a few things about myself that I hoped made me appear more interesting than I really was, my students took turns to say "interesting" things about themselves, some more so than others.

"Hi, my name is Brian. I grew up on a farm in South Carolina. I live in Chicago now, and I don't miss the farm. Well, not really. Some days, I do, kinda."

"I'm Christy, but all my friends call me CT. I'm a twin. My twin's name is also Christy, but we call her 'Ris. I'm looking forward to this class."

"Hi, I'm from Macon, Georgia. I went to elementary school, middle school, and high school in Macon. This is the first time that I've been away from my hometown. Oh, and my name is Pete."

After the introductions, in a rapid relay that sometimes made remembering the names or the "interesting" facts difficult, I introduced the subject of the class, talked about how to get a good grade, answered some questions, and that was that. Sometimes, it was my best day of the class, when a friendly spirit was still in the air and we believed in all things possible. From time to time, that spirit remained in the air, sometimes thinning, sometimes thickening, until the very last class. I had just finished such an introductory session and returned to my office, not sure what to do next. I should have left my office with a bounce in my step as if I was looking forward to the pleasures of home, but I was sort of homeless at the time. Still, I did not want to stay cooped up in my office on such a warm and airy day. It was fall, but it felt like a fairy tale season when all the elements were in perfect accord. I looked around my book-filled office and wondered if I should take a book "home." But I had books that I had taken "home" but so far had not been able to read. I spent almost all my time missing Ella and floating around my hotel room like a ghost wandering around an empty house. It was then, looking around my office a second time, that I saw the blinking light on the phone. Aha, voicemail! I thought. In my old office, I sometimes let these messages blink themselves out; they were automatically erased after a day or so of the light blinking like a single-minded traffic sign.

The very first message nearly made me ignore the rest. It was an advert promising me a free cruise if I called a certain number within the next forty-eight hours. Had telemarketers already started calling my new office line? And with an offer of a cruise – for me? I had read about all the wonderful things that happened on cruises and Joel, my best friend, loved them so much that he talked about them whenever he could. But I could not imagine myself floating on water for days if I could be somewhere on land instead. And it wasn't only because I never learned how to swim. I was simply not the type that enjoyed "floating." Even if someone paid me to, as this fellow was breathlessly offering, I would most likely not oblige. The second message was from a student who had missed the first day of class because of "health reasons." I was relieved that she was able to call and impressed that she bothered to do so. I moved on to the last message. And, suddenly, my world changed.

"Hallo, I'm Willem Kirk of Kirk and Klaus," began a measured voice, "I'm calling from Stellenbosch, South Africa on behalf of your grandfather, Mr. Ile Ka. I've been trying to reach you for some time now. It's extremely important that you call me back at this number as soon as possible..."

Mr...who? Was it "Ileka" or "Ile Ka?" My...who? Whaaat?!

I listened to the message again, then again, replaying it even slower in my mind. I listened to it many times, as if hearing it again and again would somehow further my comprehension. At some point, I looked around my office carefully, noting that I still had familiar books in familiar positions but nevertheless wondering if I was still in the same world that I had always been. Or had I somehow transited into another dimension without my intention or knowledge? Or...was this a prank? Neither Willem's voice nor the "Kirk and Klaus" suggested so. But didn't "Kirk and Klaus" also sound like a stage name? Still, Willem's voice didn't have the oiliness or giddiness of the typical marketer with a "Hello" in falsetto that always seemed to suggest that the fellow had somehow discovered the secret of the universe or wanted to share his grandmother's recipe. But if this was not a prank, then what on earth could it mean? What this voice, regardless of its measured calibration, was suggesting was impossible. My grandfather died and was buried forty-four years ago, eleven years before I was born. I knew his grave very well. Was it conceivable that he somehow – without knowing about my existence – left a message for me that took forty-four years to get to me? The idea was absurd.

So, what did this mean? Has the word "grandfather" become a newfangled code in a world fascinated by word plays? "Pass me the grandfather. Under the table, dude." "I'm angling for the grand f. Gotta aim high, bro. Only way to live." "Listen, sister, everyone is also looking for grandie. And no, I'm not gravity's uncle." But I usually kept track of that sort of thing. Should I call Willem back or would that somehow dignify what was obviously some sort of nonsensical message? What would happen next – messages from my dead parents or dear friends who have already departed? How great it would be to hear from them again. But...I had to calm myself. I should simply ignore this fellow. Maybe this was some sort of reality show, with a secret camera peeping at my every move from somewhere. Everything seemed to be a reality show these days. I looked at my office carefully, but I did not see anything that looked like a hidden camera. Perhaps that was the whole point – to hide the camera in such a fashion that I wouldn't see it. Was I becoming paranoid? I sat down again and continued staring at the phone as if some sort of clarity would somehow manifest after some time. Where was this place that this Willem fellow had called from? Stellenbosch? It sounded like a convertible or maybe a gourmet restaurant. "You want to drive my Bosch? Nice try, but that's not happening." "There's the Bosch, and then there's everything else." "Let's meet at The Stellenbosch tonight. Lordy, you mean you've never been to The Stellenbosch?" Why was my mind wandering? I shook my head, picked up the phone and called the number.

"Hallo, you've reached the office of Kirk and Klaus after our office hours. Our office hours are from 8 am to 5 pm, Monday to Friday. Your call is important to us. Please, do call us back during our office hours. Dankie."

I would later learn that, in Afrikaans, "Hallo" was "Hello" and "Dankie" meant "Thanks."

I put the phone down slowly. So, this measured voice actually came from a real person in a real office – a law firm, probably – in a real place? Since it was already past 5 pm in Stellenbosch, that meant I had to wait until Monday to clear up what must be an error. There could be no other explanation.

Perhaps, I told myself, when I finally got up to leave my office, I was focusing on the wrong word – on "grandfather" instead of "on behalf of." A call "on behalf of" my grandfather did not necessarily mean that he was no longer dead. But what did it mean then – that this fellow somehow received a message *for me* from a dead man or kept a dead man's message to himself for forty-four years? And why South Africa? Why Stellenbosch? My grandfather only left Nigeria to go to school in London, and he returned home after that. Not for the first time, I wished that my parents were still alive or that I was not an only child. I would have to call Uncle Ibe when I got home. Perhaps there was something that he could say to me, which had somehow not been said before, that would make this measured voice either deserving of measureless scorn or unbelievably worthy of attention.

Uncle Ibe probably knew more about the past than anyone else I knew. I was almost certain what his reaction would be. "It's the bogus people. Better be careful of the bogus people." For my uncle, the world was overpopulated with "bogus people" who created "problems upon problems" because they always tried "to reap where they did not sow." When he lived in the village, Ibe was like a dibia without a shrine, sometimes making ethical observations as if they were oracular pronouncements. Even with the new roads zigzagging through the village, the old Catholic church expanding every year until it seemed to have moved from the interior into the road, several American-themed restaurants and calypso beer parlors – some with flashing lights and megawatt speakers – springing up at odd corners, and all the myriad signs of a new world order, my uncle lived and laughed as if the past would never pass. He went to funerals and talked or sang about the land of the spirits, songs that people said evoked darkness, while everyone else sang hymns about the reunion in paradise. At christening ceremonies, he revived songs about the communal celebration of motherhood and childbirth that many people no longer remembered:

> Anyi bialu ile nwa ee
> Ayee
> Anyi bialu ile nwa amutalu ayi o
> Nganga kwesili ayi

And he could also dance in a fashion reminiscent of a bygone era.

As some of his colleagues in the ogba ngbada masquerade cult left to become passionate Christians or "bogus" city people, my uncle swore that the cult would never die as long as he lived. His former colleagues described the cult as "Satanic." My uncle derided their sudden ignorance. "How would they know or remember that ogba ngbada is the same brotherhood of antelope hunters that has promoted the ways of our people since the days of Ikediana, the founder of our village? The mask was how the brotherhood bridged the unknown. Ogba ngbada is in our blood."

"In whose blood?" one of his former colleagues asked him. "Better speak for yourself. How can a man go into a mask and become a spirit?"

"How does your priest raise up a chalice of wine and it becomes blood?"

I wondered: How did my uncle, who never went to church, know about the transfiguration of bread and wine into the body and blood of Jesus Christ?

"Stop wasting your time, Ibegbunam. The time for masquerades and spirits is over. It's a new world now."

"Which will be old tomorrow."

"Don't you want to go to heaven, Ibe?"

"You know what Ikediani told the missionaries when they kept trying to convert him? 'I'll come and see.' And he went to church, the only time in his life that he did so. 'Uka di n'obi,' he told the missionaries afterward. 'Religion is in the heart. May our ancestors forbid that I should forsake my fathers' shrine.'"

It baffled Ibe that anyone could ever beat the ogba ngbada drums or dance to their music and then turn his back on the brotherhood. He profoundly believed in the spirit of the masquerade, but it was the drums that possessed him. The time was never soon enough to beat the drums and marvel at the nuances of sound they were capable of, each one accenting or deepening the one before it. Ibe so loved the drums that he could hear them everywhere, even in his dreams. People warned him to beware that he did not lose his focus and fall from the palm tree one day, but he laughed at such fears. "Ogba ngbada is not the dance of death." On the occasions that the masquerade actually made an appearance, usually at the ofala festival or during the funeral of an elder, Ibe was a sight to behold – when he was not "in the spirit" – as he drummed and danced with leaping joy. He was a tall, broad-shouldered man with rippling muscles, the type of man who walked the earth as if he owned it. When he danced to the pulsing ogba ngabda drums, with the spins that he sometimes loved to perform, he seemed to become double-bodied – like a giant manifesting on earth from the misty world of legend.

My uncle now lived in Abuja, Nigeria's capital city, among "the bogus people." In his ogba ngbada days when he was still a palm wine tapper, he refused all entreaties to venture out of the village. He was unimpressed by the wealth "the bogus people" from the city came to display in the village during the Christmas or ofala festival season. He tapped his wine, drank quite a bit, savored local delicacies, promoted the ogba ngbada brotherhood, and whistled about the village – or loafed about, as my aunt would say – as if he was the happiest man on earth. And he possibly was until his elder sister, my aunt, evacuated him from the village.

Unlike my uncle, my aunt, Rosette – her own version of her baptismal name, Rose – believed in "modernity." She was a medium-built woman with dimples that softened her face when she smiled – like a cascade of sunshine on a platter of butter. She didn't smile often, but when she did it was a sight to behold. Even when she did not, she was still a beautiful woman whose size belied her boundless energy. She confessed that our local cuisine remained her guilty pleasure; otherwise, she went to church every Sunday, had no time for ogba ngbada or many of the things that my uncle cared about. In fact, she rarely visited the village. She lived in Abuja, where she was "a contractor of everything," as my uncle described her – from urban sanitation to road construction in remote villages. Despite their differences, the two of them were quite friendly toward each other and never forgot that they were brother and sister. Whenever Ibe got in trouble, my aunt always rushed to his aid as swiftly as possible. Eventually, she began to ask him to leave the village and come and live in Abuja.

"The village has nothing to offer you. You can't just stay here wasting away. Only God knows why you insist on being a palm wine tapper when you don't have to."

"Is that how you see it?" Ibe queried. "I'm not wasting away. You want me to leave my father's house, my house, and come and stay in *your* house in the city so that you and your husband will turn me into your houseboy?"

"Surely, you know me better than that, Ibe. You're my brother."

"Of course, but..."

"My husband is hardly there anyway. He's a pilot, as you know. And you only have to stay with us until you know your way around."

"Still..."

"OK, you can rent and furnish your own apartment. I can help if you want me to. Father bequeathed his wealth to us, so why are you living like this?"

"Thanks, but there's no need for that. I have everything that I need here, and I like tapping wine. The village is in my blood."

"Ogba ngbada is in your blood. The village is in your blood. Everything is in your blood. Only you, Ibe. What is the matter with you?"

Ibe would not budge. My aunt made all sorts of promises, even subtle threats, but it was obvious that my uncle had no intention of ever leaving the village – until the accidental intervention of Pastor Isaiah of the Jesus Jesus or Double J Church.

No one knew where Isaiah came from, although the tale later spread that he had been a worker in the vineyard of the eclectic Pastor White in Fegge, a riverside town, before some sort of disagreement made him decide to start his own church. He was a clean-shaven young man with the sort of sparkling white teeth that was seen only in toothpaste commercials. He wore a flowing white garment with a large cross as a necklace and carried a bell that appeared as big as his sizable head. He did not stop in our village but passed through to the nearby town, which was bigger and busier.

"The days of crying in the wilderness are over," he cried. "This is the age of miracles. Blessed be the name of the Lord. Blessed be he who comes in the name of the Lord."

He often burst into his favorite hymn, bellowing it as if its power lay in how noisily he could sing it:

Let the spirit of the Lord come down
Let the spirit of the Lord from heaven come down
Let the spirit of the Lord come down

As he sang, tears sometimes coursed down his cheeks as if he was a new messiah overburdened by both the old and new sins of the world. The song was usually the prelude to a "miracle hour" that beckoned to the afflicted from near and distant places. He seemed able to perform all sorts of miracles – to make the lame walk, make the barren conceive in triples, make the dumb speak, make the divorced reconcile, even make dunces appear like geniuses in their examination grades. His fame spread quickly and people came from everywhere to see him. The villages around his church, including ours, entered into a boom era.

"Power pass power," people said. "Pastor Isaiah power na double power."

"Triple"

"No, four-ple."

"Countless. The power too much."

The adulation overpowered stories that his power was not "of God" but was "a very strong juju" that he had sacrificed his entire family to gain. Those who peddled this story pointed out that the "man of God" who reconciled couples and made barren women fruitful had neither a wife nor children. "Why e no help himself first before e dey help others?" they asked. Pastor Isaiah's advocates retorted that he was still a young man and would surely get married and start a family "in God's own time." Whatever the source of Pastor Isaiah's power, it seemed boundless and he was willing to test it against other sorts of power. First, he took on the Catholic Church, railing from his pulpit that "orthodox Christians, Catholics in particular" worshiped a God of the There and Then. "But the God that I serve is of the Here and Now." His congregation roared in assent as they did in response to everything that he said. My uncle scoffed that if Pastor Isaiah told his church members that they were all unredeemable bastards they would still roar in assent and even speak in tongues for good measure. But no one listened to Ibe. "You heathen," they told him. "Better repent before the Rapture, otherwise you'll burn and gnash your teeth in hell forever and ever." However, there was something about this division into a God of the There and Then and a God of the Here and Now that puzzled some of the congregants, especially those who remembered hearing the same Pastor Isaiah declaim that God was "indivisible, unchangeable, timeless, immemorial" and all the other bountiful descriptors that he was capable of conjuring. Isaiah explained to these "doubters" that God was "not a man that He would ever change," but that "orthodox Christians" worshiped Him as if He was the God of the There and Then; the fault therefore was in their approach to "the Divine Emmanuel, the Timeless Shepherd." The congregants roared enough to almost deafen the villages nearby.

"They limit God because they approach Him as if His holiness and capacity and blessings and mercy are not infinite. But we, we are the sons and daughters of the Trinity, children of the Kingdom, and we will not whisper for miracles as if they might not come to pass; no, we will proclaim our miracles and claim them because the God of Hallelujah has given us the right to bless ourselves."

To hear Pastor Isaiah was affecting enough. To see him

speaking like a possessed being with his eyes shut and his bodily motions – from his pomaded hair to his wingtip shoes – in rhythmic gyration gradually began to drain other nearby churches and to fill the Jesus Jesus Church. People came to be healed or simply to witness the riveting performance.

After deriding the Catholic Church, Pastor Isaiah decided on something more daring. He announced that he had decided to wipe out – "to demystify, atrophy, disintegrate, excommunicate" – all the "pagan shrines" in the villages surrounding his church. An uneasy silence rippled through the church before the church members began to roar as always. Some of them, especially those who still visited these shrines in secret, worried in their hearts that this might be a step too far.

"I want to show you that these so-called gods are all man-made, pieces of wood and rags that fools bow down to as divine entities. God has asked me to tell you that He will especially bless any believer who demonstrates His power by wiping out these blights on the face of the earth."

That was all he needed to say. A posse headed by a former masquerade-carrier, who had since changed his name from Cheta to Isaiah, Jr., quickly organized itself and ran around the villages burning down shrines that had been there longer than anyone could remember. They called it The Cleansing or Holy Isaiah Fire. Anyone who tried to stop them, including priests and priestesses who until recently were revered or dreaded voices of these ancient deities, was beaten mercilessly. When this posse showed up to burn down both the shrine of Ani, the earth goddess, in front of the ogba ngbada hut and the hut itself, an enraged Ibe told them that that would only happen over his dead body.

"As you wish," Isaiah, Jr. said to him, and motioned his group forward.

Ibe was bigger than every one of them but he only managed to bring down a few before they battered him as if he was a piece of boiled yam in a mortar. They were not satisfied even then and tried to drag him into the masquerade hut before they set it ablaze. Some villagers intervened. Roofed with raffia palms and with a plenitude of dry material within, both the shrine and the masquerade hut were like tinders. Their swift combustion was a confirmation to the posse that the two places were indeed homes of the devil. "See how dem dey burn like Satan headquarters. Holy Ghost, fire! Fire them well well."

After Ibe recovered, he could not bear the sight of the burned shrine and masquerade hut. The villagers advised him that the gods were capable of fighting for themselves, so he should forget the experience and move on with his life. Ibe appeared to listen, but there was something that kept pushing him to strike a blow in return. And whatever it was propelled him all the way to the headquarters of the Jesus Jesus Church. He managed to get to the front row, but when he attempted to jump onto the dais and confront Pastor Isaiah, his bodyguards seized him. That was the last that anyone saw Ibe for a long time. It would not be the first time that dissidents had disappeared in Pastor Isaiah's church never to be seen or heard from again.

Ibe's savior was Aunt Rosette and her "bogus connections." Ibe had been missing for more than a week before my aunt came visiting. When she heard the story, she was outraged that the villagers had not made more vigorous attempts to contact her even though she had just returned from a trip abroad. She made a call and truckloads of policemen came to accompany her to the Jesus Jesus Church. Pastor Isaiah vanished before the policemen got there. A starved and delirious Ibe was discovered naked and filth-encrusted in a dungeon beneath the dais on which Pastor Isaiah often performed his "power miracles." My aunt evacuated Ibe from the village without a fight and perhaps without his knowledge.

Pastor Isaiah returned a few weeks later and said he had gone to the wilderness on a planned retreat to recharge. His congregation roared, as if the incident concerning Ibe never happened. Shortly afterward, Isaiah, Jr. died in a strange road accident right in front of one of the shrines he had burned down. The car he was traveling in seemed to career off the road for no reason and then travel half a mile or so before ramming into a tree in front of where the shrine used to be. Everyone in the vehicle survived without any injury except Isaiah, Jr. Some of the villagers whispered that the gods were still alive after all. Pastor Isaiah scoffed at such notions.

"What gods? There is only one God – the Great I Am That I Am, His Holy Holiness, His Divine Divinity, Yah Yahweh, Jehovah Jireh, Amen Emmanuel, His Excellent Excellency. If the gods are alive – what a silly notion! – they should come for me and then we shall see who is alive and who is dead."

Nothing happened to him, so his church members began to call him Invincible Isaiah.

Meanwhile, Ibe found settling in the city even more difficult than leaving the village. He was in uncharted territory. He had stopped going to school after two years in high school, insisting that that was "enough *oyibo* education" for him. He found himself poorly prepared to live in the city and began to plot returning to the village, so my aunt forced him to go back to school despite his age and finish a high school education that he had never cared for. Something must have happened to Ibe in his second year or so because he suddenly started to take his education seriously. He passed his final exams and even went on to the university, an accomplishment that no one other than my aunt had thought possible. My aunt helped him get a job, but my uncle didn't last long in that position. "I'm not an office person" was his explanation after he simply stopped going to work.

Through his successes and tribulations, my uncle never forgot the village. He was like a reluctant sailor consoled by the fact that no matter how vast the sea it always ends in sand. He was therefore especially pained when he finally visited the village many years later and discovered that people had begun to look at him as one of the "bogus" people. The "madness of Isaiah," as Ibe described Pastor Isaiah's ministry, was over. The pastor was discovered dead one morning at the spot where the shrine of the earth goddess used to be. The "invincible" pastor had gone to bed in his "official quarters" the previous evening only for his corpse to be discovered about seven miles away the next morning without any explanation. Ibe pondered the story but made no comment. He contemplated staying back in the village but realized to his shock that he had become wary of trees. Every time he tried to climb one, a warning signal went off in his head about all the things that could go wrong – the sort of possibilities that he had not considered once upon a time. So, he returned to Abuja and started a restaurant specializing in African cuisine. "Everywhere in Abuja, you have all these bogus restaurants that sell fancy food with musical names. Not Muoma." It was just like my uncle to name his restaurant Muoma rather than Angel, but it was also surprising that he chose to do so. He was a man who still cared deeply about the old ways in a world that he said had "transformed like faded cloth."

My uncle was quite a character, but he paled – like everyone and everything else – in comparison to his father, my grandfather.

My grandfather was "the biggest masquerade" that everyone in my village had ever known. That was how my uncle described him. People talked about him so much that I often felt I was unfortunate to have arrived eleven years after his passage. Even though I never met him, he was an unforgettable figure in my mind. People spoke about him as if he was some sort of superman, a legend in his own lifetime. Some people said he came out of the forest; others said he came out of the night. I never understood what they meant. Forest. Night. They almost made him seem like a spirit.

My mother would shake her head and say "Your grandfather, ha!" as if she lacked the words to begin to describe him.

"Your grandfather wasn't just a man," my father would attempt to elaborate, "he was a phenomenon."

"Why," I sometimes asked, "did this phenomenon – who was also the best rainmaker that anyone had ever seen or heard of – die so young?"

"Because death is not a masquerade, but it eats away or even yanks off the raffia of the masquerade until it unmasks it. I miss Father very much, but if a masquerade stays too long in the arena it transforms from a spirit into a man."

"You're sounding like Uncle Ibe."

"Why not? He's my brother, and we're all sons of Ileka."

And I am his grandson.

When the spirits came out of the forest, they became masks; when the masks sink to the ground, they become men.

I drove home, mostly by instinct, but I arrived safely. Home at the time was an extended stay hotel that I had checked into two-and-a-half weeks ago while I hunted for a house. It was something I should have done earlier, but I didn't. Maybe that was why that Willem fellow, if he was speaking the truth, had been unable to find me earlier. I had changed cities and jobs, moving from a community college in Houston to a university outside Memphis. Even before I left Houston, I had legally changed my last name. I had been named after my grandfather at birth and people often said that I was his reincarnation, an observation that I always considered a great honor. Some of these observers pointed out that, except Uncle Ibe, everyone else in the family was medium-sized but I was built like a prizefighter, just like my grandfather. My first name was my grandfather's first name, and my last name was my grandfather's last name. I wanted to include my father's personal name in my list of names; so, I started using my grandfather's last name as my middle name and my father's middle name as my last name. I am not sure that this decision would have pleased even my father, but it was mine to make.

Living apart from Ella, even for a few weeks, was taking a toll on me. We had been together for five years but only got married last year. She was the reason I stayed back in America after four years in graduate school. I was set to return home after defending my dissertation and I had started making departure arrangements when Ella moved in next door. I lived then in an apartment complex close to the university that teemed with graduate students. I did not know many of them well, except for the occasional meetings in the laundromat or the hallway. My neighbor, Idris, the fellow who used to live in the apartment next door, was from Sudan, and he had moved to New York to take up a tenure-track job. We used to converse occasionally, but it was never more than "How are you today? What's happening in Sudan these days?" "Oh, Sudan will be fine, someday. What about Nigeria?" "Still more oil than sense, unfortunately." We would laugh and part. Then, one day, he invited me to a party. It was so unexpected. We ran into each other in the hallway and he asked me whether I had any engagements that evening. "It's me o," I said jovially. "When did we start speaking this fancy English? 'Engagements' indeed." He laughed. "But you're the one in the English department. I was only trying to impress you." He then invited me to a birthday party. For some reason, I didn't ask him whose birthday it was and his relationship to the person. I accepted because I was bored and I had never been to a Sudanese birthday party.

It turned out to be an odd night. We arrived at the venue without any presents and went and sat in a corner. Everyone there was either white or African American, as far as I could tell. Where were our Sudanese hosts or co-guests? I wondered. Nobody greeted us warmly, and Idris barely greeted anyone. But he was quite nimble about replenishing our food and drinks. We sat there eating and drinking and nursing a slow-moving, sometimes tottering, conversation. At some point, I began to get the uneasy feeling that we had crashed the party. People looked at us strangely, and there were a few times that someone began to make their way toward us with a determined expression and then probably decide that we were not worth the bother. I didn't want to get into a quarrel or a fight, especially that sort, so I prompted Idris and we left sooner than he had intended.

After that night, I stayed away from Idris, and I didn't know when he moved out. I was on my way back to my apartment one evening when I heard his door opening. I turned around, wondering if he would recognize me if I straightened myself to appear taller. Thankfully, I did not, because the person I saw emerge from his room was like an apparition. What was this sparkling woman – well-toned body, beautifully coiffured hair, glorious buttocks, sassy walk – doing in Idris's apartment? We passed each other without a word, although she looked me up and down. After that day, I began to pay attention to that apartment like never before, and it did not take me long to realize that Idris must have moved out and Miss Sparkling was my new neighbor.

Until then, I had been saying airily that I had taken everything America had to offer and I was ready to go home. I wasn't too sure anymore, so I decided I needed a bit of "American experience." It was the sort of thing that would have kept me awake at night, but it didn't. "Journeys end in lovers meeting," Shakespeare had written in a moment of inspiration in a lifetime of inspirations. She was my journey's end. My heart fluttered as if it had learned to waltz. I deferred my return until next year, and I told anyone who asked that my American education would be incomplete without American experience. "One complements the other." I didn't think it would sound sensible if I said I had decided to stay back because I saw a vision in the hallway that I knew next to nothing about. This must be love, I told myself. But...was it love? Could it be love? Fortunately, I got an adjunct teaching position, so I didn't have to worry about a job for at least one year. But I rarely saw Miss Sparkling. She seemed to come back in the middle of the night and leave before I woke up. That made no sense. What sort of schedule was that? What was I to do – follow her? Of course not. Then, what?

The additional year that I gave myself was half-gone and I still had not spoken to Miss Sparkling. I was under growing pressure from my father to come home. So, I decided to do something almost desperate. I bought a scented card and I wrote on it "I don't want to wait twenty-seven years living next door to 'Alice'. No. 44." I had become like a character in an old song, "Living Next Door to Alice." I slipped the card under her door. I must have fallen asleep waiting for her to come home. A persistent knock on my door woke me up.

"Who's that?" I asked with more confidence than I felt.

"Open the door, No. 44. It's Alice."

I opened the door, and Miss Sparkling walked in, smiling mischievously.

"You're supposed to be waiting for me with candle lights, the whole works."

"Sorry, I fell asleep."

"I've been wondering when you'd make your move. And how. The *how* is always important. I thought maybe we'd run into each other at the laundromat."

I was rather confused because this was not the way that I thought she would react. I wasn't even sure how I expected her to react. "I don't understand," I finally said. "How did you know I was going to make a move?"

"I saw the way you looked at me the very first time, and I've been watching you."

"How? I've never seen you."

"Sure, but I've seen you."

"Why were you watching me?"

"I kind of like you too, but it'll never work between us. So, stop getting ideas. Have a good night."

"What do you mean..."

She was gone. I rubbed my eyes to make sure that I was not asleep. If I was awake, then what was the meaning of all that? She knocked at my door at 2 am to tell me that she kind of liked me but that she would never date me? I suppose that was the point where I should have firmed my travel plans and walked away philosophically, but I was like a bull in the ring and I had already seen the matador whip around the red cape. I charged, but not with murder in my eyes. I was in love or perhaps in lust. Whatever it was, I went out and bought packs of scented cards.

Several cards later, sometimes two in one day, with many unattributed quotes, she finally agreed to go on "one dinner, not a date" with me "just to talk." I should have been happy, but there were so many qualifications attached to her agreement that I didn't know what to make of it. Still, I was seeing more of her these days than I did in my first six months of deferment.

I rarely ate out, so choosing a restaurant to take Ella or Emmanuella – I now knew her name – wasn't an easy decision. I finally chose an "inn" that I often passed on my way to work for no other reason than that the place was tastefully colorful and I often heard laughter and a delicious aroma wafting from its interior.

"Nice choice," she said as a waitress ushered us to a table. "Looks like you did your research well."

"Thanks."

She only glanced at the menu before making a detailed order, as if she ate out frequently.

"I'll have the same thing," I said when the waitress asked me what I wanted.

Ella smiled.

"Why are you punishing me?" I asked her.

"The question should be: Why are you stalking me?

You're lucky you're Nigerian like me, otherwise I would have called the police. But, Nigerian or not, your obsession needs to stop. I'm serious."

"Forgive me for pestering you, but I'm not sure I can stop. You know, I would understand if you didn't like me at all or if you had a boyfriend. Maybe you do, but I've never seen you with anyone. To be honest, I don't ever see you, but sometimes I can hear you in your apartment."

"So, you've been listening through the wall?"

"It's an old building. It doesn't keep secrets well."

"What do you hear?"

"You must like music a lot, all sorts."

"I'm in the music department, my third year as a PhD student. But I like music a lot anyway. That's why I'm in the music department. And you...why do you shout on the phone in the middle of the night sometimes?"

"Oh, sorry about that. I'm not really shouting, but my father wants me to come home – that's Nigeria – immediately."

"Are you a prince somewhere, and the kingdom is in danger because of your absence?"

"You like to joke. I love that. No, I'm not a prince, but it's a family tradition. We always return home after going to school abroad. Both my grandfather and my father did."

"Family tradition. Impressive. So, why are you deviating from it? You finished last year."

"I'm staying back for practical training."

"Are you a scientist?"

"No, but..."

"Let's cut to the chase. I kind of like you. There's something about you that gets to me. But I'm done with Nigerian men. You only want one thing, and you can't wait to scramble out the door once you get it. So, please don't send me another card after tonight."

"But that's what all men do, not just Nigerian men, all men of a certain kind."

"And you're different?"

"No, I'm not different. I've also made that scramble out the door in the past, but I was in those relationships from the beginning for only one thing. This time, it's different. It's different because you've already made me so. Don't ask me to explain because I don't even understand it."

"This is the point where I'm supposed to melt into your arms, right? I know you're PhD English, so of course you know your rhetoric."

"How can I get you to understand that this is not a game for me? It's my only mission now."

"I'm a mission?"

"You know what I mean."

"Sorry, but I don't trust Nigerian men. They lie so much that they will tell a lie for a peck when they can get a kiss with the truth."

Ella had embraced Nigeriana, especially the Nigerian community in Houston, when she arrived to begin her doctoral study, like a parched desert rejoicing at the sight of an oasis. Unlike me, she was born in America, in Wyoming, and Houston was an eye-opening exposure to "the Nigerian homeland abroad." She had a full scholarship for the first year, so that gave her the chance to attend the countless activities that kept the community throbbing – town union meetings, alma mater parties, ethnic union inaugurations, birthday parties, graduation parties, wedding ceremonies, wakes, "diaspora visits" from wealthy or touring Nigerians, summer picnics, receptions, visitations, church luncheons, friendship associations. It didn't take long before she got into a relationship that ended or began to totter after she agreed to spend the night in her boyfriend's apartment. She had thought that it was a "real" relationship, so she was both dazed and heartbroken. Her "boyfriend," a pharmacist, stopped answering her calls and even denied any knowledge of her when she finally confronted him – already making a public appearance with another woman – at a birthday party. "Na by force?" he asked her. "I don't know you." She then decided to focus on her studies. She had to anyway because she needed to get a job since her scholarship in her second and third years only covered her tuition but did not guarantee her any stipend. She went to school during the day and to work in the evenings, which was why I hardly saw her. On Sundays, the only free day she had during the week, she was often too tired to leave her apartment. But, tired or not, it was the day she had to do her laundry and prepare for the new week.

"That character, my so-called boyfriend, put me off Nigerian men. He chased me as if I was nirvana, then dropped me like rotten fruit. I thought he was enlightened, but I should have known better."

"You can't let someone like that redefine who you are. And I'm not a hunter in that sense. You're my last bus stop, as we say in Nigeria."

"Meaning?"

"I love you, only you."

"You love me, already? Aren't you moving too fast?"

"It's true. It's true today. It'll always be true."

Despite her reservations, I must have said something that night that touched her. She eventually agreed to go on a date with me, and that was the beginning of a beautiful relationship. She graduated the next year and got a tenure-track job as an assistant professor. We moved in together. Like most things that we did, we didn't spend forever discussing it. It seemed like the right thing to do, so we did it. But there was something that we did first.

"I better tell you this before we start living together," she told me then. "I can hardly cook, but I'll learn if it's important to you."

"Of course, I know you can't cook. I'll teach you if you want to learn."

"You can really cook?"

"I've cooked for you before, haven't I? And you enjoyed the meal and licked your lips."

"You!" she said with a smile. "I thought that maybe you were putting on a show."

"The food was real."

"And delicious. But I never saw you actually cooking it."

"You! Well, I can cook. My mom made sure of that."

"You see why mothers are special. Now it's your turn. Is there something you want to tell me about yourself, something I should know?"

I didn't know how to begin.

"Come on, Ile, silence is not a good response right now."

"There's something I've been meaning to tell you, but I don't want to lose you."

She looked at me and smiled with a mischievous glint in her eyes. "Cut out the act. You think you can scare me off and then I'll let you go? Not a chance."

"No, I'm serious. I have an anger disorder."

"That's it, your big secret?"

"I mean I've got a really devilish temper. It's worse than anything you can imagine."

She started laughing but fell silent, maybe because of the look on my face. She looked at me carefully, almost squinting, as if she was seeing me for the first time. "You, temper? How's that possible?"

"It's on my record."

"You, record? Did you kill someone?"

"No, but I could have."

"Is this a joke? You better stop because it's no longer

funny, if it ever was."

"I've never been more serious in my life."

"But I've never ever heard you raise your voice."

"That's the point. I don't have a temper every day or even every year. I could go on for years without any incident and then something happens and I can't control myself. At all. I don't know how to describe what happens, but it seems that I first hear what sounds like the high-pitched whistle of a passing train, then something that sounds like thundering waves, and I see all these abstract patterns transforming themselves with dizzying acceleration in front of me – all these things happening almost simultaneously – and it's like I'm in a blinding fog. I end up doing some terrible things. It's happened three times, and it frightens me to death. I feel myself changing and I fight to hold down my anger, but something overpowers me and by the time I regain myself I've done something horrible. I've seen all kinds of specialists, but they can't quite figure out what is wrong with me – how I can go for seven to ten years being normal and then lose it completely over something that I've probably dealt with quite reasonably in the past."

It was as if I had doused a bucket of ice-cold water on her, and it was the first time I had ever seen that mischievous glint in her eyes extinguished. "I love you, Ile," she said slowly, "but now I'm really worried. So, this means you could kill me one day and then cry about it later?"

"I'll never hurt you, you know that."

"Not anymore. You just told me that you can't control yourself during these...incidents. Take a look at yourself. You could easily crush me to death before any help arrives, if ever."

"I've been to rehab and taken anger management classes. I think I'm much better now than before. There's been no incident since."

"When was the last time?"

"Four years ago, my third year in America."

"So, this thing is likely to manifest again in three to six years?"

"I hope not."

"What happened the last time?"

"I went with a friend, a colleague, to a hotel bar near the campus to celebrate something or the other. I think we had just finished our PhD coursework. The idea was to have two beers and then go home. It was a small bar, so you could easily hear what was being said at the next table. There were two guys at the next table, and they were arguing about something. Even though I didn't mean to listen, I soon figured out that one of them had just returned from Uganda and was telling his friend what a beautiful place Africa is. 'Never mind what you see on the news. Of course, there are bad things going on there, like everywhere else in the world. But it's still a fine place.' His friend scoffed and then said rather loudly, as if he wanted us to hear clearly 'Don't be carried away. There's nothing good about Africa. There has never been. As a historian, can you mention one thing, one thing, that's good about African culture?' That's all I remember. I'm told I pounced on that man and beat him so savagely that he spent some time in hospital."

"But that doesn't make any sense. You attacked someone because he said something to someone else about Africa, not about you? Did you ever think that people everywhere, even in Africa, are likely to talk about Africa as if it's Disneyland?"

"That's the point. I'm used to all the talk about Africa, and have been for a long time. I don't know what happened that day, and that's what's unsettling. I was very lucky that the man I attacked worked in the attorney general's office and was planning to run for state congress. He didn't want to be tagged a racist by the press, so he helped suppress the details of the case, but I still got a suspended sentence for a misdemeanor."

"What was the first incident?"

"I was nine, and I got into a heated argument with my best friend about whose mother was the better cook. In a fit of anger, I cut deep into his foot with a machete. It was a wonder I did not sever the foot. He spent a long time in the hospital and he still has an ugly mark on his foot until this day."

"Jesus Christ! God in heaven! You really did that?"

"Sadly, yes. That almost brought permanent enmity between the two families, but our parents eventually reconciled after my father made a significant settlement. I think my friend's parents agreed to the settlement in the first place because of who my grandfather was."

A deep silence fell between us.

"Please, say something," I pleaded.

"What am I supposed to say? That the thing I thought was a rose is actually a thorn?"

"No, all that is in the past."

"For now."

Another echoing silence.

"And I was so happy," she said with a hint of tears in her eyes. "Why is life like this?"

"Listen, Ella..."

"You have to go, Ile, please. I need to think."

"Ella..."

"Just go!"

That was how the relationship would have ended if not for Beth, Ella's twin. They were not identical. Ella was prettier, but Beth was more vivacious. She had an unforgettable presence and a bubbly optimism like someone who knew that the world had its dark spots but that they were not so dark that they diminished or defied its brightness. "This is the one," she told Ella the first day she met me. "I like him." It was an important compliment because it did not take me long to figure out that Beth was probably the only person capable of convincing Ella to change her mind once it was made up. Ella apparently had the same sort of influence over Beth.

I ran crying to Beth, but she too was shocked by my story. "This is bad, really bad," she said. My heart sank. I had never heard her talk like that. I was used to her playfulness and breezy laughter, like an adult who truly had not forgotten what it means to be a child. However, she eventually promised to talk to her sister. "Maybe I shouldn't, but I still believe in you. I just hope I'm not making a mistake." I don't know what she said to Ella, but she agreed to take me back if I consented to go and see a psychiatrist with her.

"Certainly," I said. "We should."

The psychiatrist she chose was a TV personality who presented a program on "total healing." He was English American, he often said, referring to the fact that he had moved his practice to Houston from London only a few years ago. His name was Joel and he was the sort of charmer who believed in his own charms. I liked him so much that we soon became friends.

After he listened to me tell my story and Ella express her fears, Joel advised us that the practical thing for us to do was to go for anger management classes as a couple regularly. That way, I'd continually relearn "the keys of self-control" and Ella would know what to watch out for and what to do if necessary.

"The other option is to prescribe medication, but I'm not sure there's effective medication for something that happens once in seven to ten years and which seems to take a different form each time."

Joel always seemed so proper and professional on TV and in his consulting room, with his shirt buttoned to the neck and tucked in, his British accent well-groomed and his general appearance well-cultivated, that I was surprised when I ran into him on Beale Street, Memphis's naughtiest street. I wasn't aware that he had planned to travel out of Houston that week. He was in Memphis for a conference. I was in the city for a different conference. He appeared slightly drunk and disheveled, but he invited me back to the bar he was just coming from in an accent that sounded more American than British. I hesitated, but he practically pulled me along. We were about the same height, but I was heavier. Was this the same Joel we had gone to see or was he, like Ella, a twin? I wondered. But how would his twin know who I was? There was a pianist playing the biggest piano I had ever seen, but that bar was probably one of the few places that you could speak and be heard in Beale Street with its rows of colorful nightclubs and bars that made it "one of the most iconic streets in America" as well as "the birthplace of rock and roll."

"What are you doing here?" he asked me.

"I have the same question for you. I'm here for a conference. But everyone comes to or passes through Beale Street at one time or the other."

He smiled as if he had just made a discovery that pleased him. "I like you."

He ordered a cocktail. I asked for a beer.

"Are you American?" I asked the question that his new accent kept prompting.

"Oh, my accent. No, I'm British, but I've been here now for five years and I've learned to speak with this middle-of-the-ocean accent. It relaxes me."

"But on TV..."

"The producers say my British accent is good for the ratings. Fortunately, I've not lost it. So, it's my business accent. But this is Beale Street, man, perhaps the world's most colorful cruise. Unfortunately, it's not seaborne."

"You like cruises?"

"I love them, and I've been on so many that I've almost lost count. I once sailed on a mini metropolis with more than five thousand people around the Caribbean. It was the most beautiful experience imaginable. Have you ever been on a cruise?"

"No, and it's unlikely I'll ever go on one."

"What a loss."

That was one of the things that made Joel such good company. There was never any sense of arrogance, the sort you would expect from a TV personality. He spoke freely and he listened to whatever I had to say; whenever our views diverged, he would say something like "What a loss" and move on to the next subject. After we returned to Houston, I began to associate with him whenever I could, which was not as often as I would have liked because I was not sure how Ella would react to the idea of me drinking frequently with our psychiatrist.

"Do you do this with your patients often?" I asked Joel.

"Do what?"

"Run into them on the street and invite them to the bar."

"Of course not. But you're not my patient. You came to me and I referred you elsewhere. And I didn't just run into you on the street. I ran into you on *Beale* Street. It seemed like the right thing to do. I follow my instincts."

My friendship with Joel was a new beginning for him that he had started to believe might never come. Even though he was evidently successful – a TV personality who was fairly well-known for preaching the gospel of "total healing" as well as for his successful practice – Joel still bled, or so it seemed, from an old wound. "No matter how well a deep wound heals," he told me, "the scar always remains." Joel believed in friendships, so much so that it was his religion. "That's all I cared about. I didn't go to church, but I very well understood the story of Christ dying on the cross for us because I would have done the same for my friends – or friend. My elder sister, who had the good sense to believe in a true religion, used to advise me to put my faith in God, not 'the things of the world. The world is no good. God will never fail you, but the world always will.'" Joel discountenanced her "religiosity." He had a best friend, Smith, whose friendship was so dear to him that he would have forsaken the whole world, including his dear sister, for his sake – until he walked in on Smith and his girlfriend, Rita, in bed. Suddenly, all those seemingly innocent signs of affection from Smith toward Rita took on a new meaning. Something had been afoot all the time, but he had misread the signs.

Joel was so shocked that something went wrong in his brain; he had a seizure right there. The doctors initially feared that the seizure would result in some form of paralysis or brain damage, especially when their patient began to mechanically mutter questions like "How is it fair that a bird can fly but a man can't?" or "Why does it rain without sunshine?" But Joel recovered – "in body mostly," according to him. When he left the hospital, all he could think about was how to kill himself. In what sort of world did friends do that sort of thing to each other? He did not want to be part of that world. His sister suspected his intention and began to watch him closely. "Even when I went to the bathroom, she stayed outside the door and spoke to me about the blood of the Savior. It was the first time that I began to appreciate why religion is probably the best invention in the world. You know why? Because the world is otherwise just a cavernous sinkhole with 'humans' who don't even know what it means to be human. Immanuel Kant was right: 'Out of the crooked timber of humanity, no straight thing can be made.' I had a degree in psychiatry, but I'm not sure I really understood the human mind, what it's capable of, until then."

Joel eventually decided to relocate to America. "My heart no longer bleeds, but even after all these years the pain is sometimes still palpable. I think that betrayal deserves a different kind of hellfire." I was Joel's first "real friend" since then. "There's something about you," he said to me with that goofy smile that sometimes lit up his face. "I can sense that you're a real person, and I've not had that feeling since God knows when."

Meanwhile, my reunion with Ella had not quite gone the way I hoped. Something seemed to have evaporated from our relationship, and I had to woo her a second time. It took about three months before she agreed that I could move in with her and maybe another three months before she started sleeping well with me beside her. And then something happened, something so terrible that it made the ears tingle.

The fish said that it is because it lives in water that it understands the language of the waves.

Beneath the euphoria promoted by the unending orgy of Nigerian parties in Houston was a kind of sadness. It wasn't simply that people appeared to have something nasty to say about other people once their backs were turned, but the ultimate expression of the loving spirit promoted by these parties – marriages – never seemed to last. Once upon a time, Nigerian marriages were cast in stone; these days, in Houston, they often lasted only long enough for the couple to batter and shame each other.

"Why marry when you'll soon leave him anyway?" one of Ella's friends asked, perhaps in anticipation of our engagement and marriage. "Our men are so useless."

"But you're married, Ioma, aren't you?"

"For now. I'm watching him closely," she said with a laugh.

"Ioma" was her friend's American version of her birth name, Ifeoma. Her husband was a self-described multimillionaire, "one of the richest Africans in America." He owned some sort of healthcare business but sprayed dollar bills at Nigerian parties as if he had a private money mine.

"Are you sure other men are better? Our divorce rate is not the highest in the world."

"OK o, do not say I didn't warn you."

"What's going on in this world?" Ella wondered after she

left. "Do women everywhere think their men are worse than other men?"

"Why ask me? You used to think like that."

"That's true – maybe, maybe not – until a certain No. 44 started talking to Alice by slipping cards under my apartment door."

We both laughed.

"Most of my tirade against Nigerian men was just a front. That's the truth. I fell for you right from the beginning."

"You think I didn't know that?"

"Look at you!"

We started laughing again.

"My friends ask me these days what I'm still doing with my husband," complained a caterer who became Ella's friend when she was still an active member of the Nigerian community. "It's as if I should be ashamed that I'm married to the same man after thirty years."

These separations occurred for several reasons, and from time to time the couple were able to resolve their differences – sometimes with the intervention of their families back in Nigeria – and come back together. The reconciliation process, both the ones that worked and the ones that failed, was often facilitated by Alhaji, who owned the largest "African store" in Houston. He came to Houston from Ogbomosho in the 1970s, when it was quite an event for a Nigerian to travel abroad, usually to study. Alhaji managed to stay in college long enough to graduate, then he married a white woman he met in the prison service where he got a job as a counselor. But it was as if he lacked the ability to counsel himself. In three years, he went through three marriages – one white, one black, and one Asian – then he sent a message to his mother in Ogbomosho to help him find a wife "with good home training." He was lucky because other Nigerians would later try to do the same thing only to discover that a woman did not make an ideal partner simply because she was raised in Ogbomosho or in Houston. Alhaji's luck netted him the woman of his dreams, to whom he had stayed married for more than thirty years. Many Nigerians did not know about Alhaji's failed marriages, so they saw him as an example of the ideal husband, which his wife assured everyone he was. His long stay in America made him one of the oldest Nigerians around, both in age and in the experience of Americana. He was also respected because of the way he carried himself. Alhaji did not attend all the Nigerian celebrations and wakes, but when he did he never drank alcohol; he pecked at the food as if he was only doing so to honor the hosts; he donated generously; and he danced – if at all – like an egungun masquerade making a ritual oscillation. All these enhanced people's perception of him.

But the factor that elevated Alhaji above everybody else was the size of his "African store" – the grocery store that sold all sorts of African and Caribbean imports from chin chin to Icelandic stockfish to black soap to Brazilian hair. When Nigerians began to arrive in Houston in large numbers, Alhaji had reckoned that the number made a new market not only necessary but imperative. "More people, more mouths, more pockets," he told his wife. He retired from the prison service and started the only "African store" that sometimes sold foodstuffs to needy customers on credit. People joked that a large number of Nigerians in Houston either owed money to Alhaji or had done so in the past or will do so in the future. It was only a matter of time before some of these people began to bring their domestic problems for him to help them resolve. He was willing to listen and counsel. Sometimes, he managed to rejoin separated couples. Sometimes, even his best efforts did not ensure a reconciliation.

"Marriage is deep," he told his wife, "and some of these issues don't make any sense. A man wants to leave his wife because she wore a fine dress to a party, which he thinks was for the purpose of attracting other men. What am I supposed to say to her – to wear rags the next time? Or a woman wants to leave her husband because he ate the Angus beef that she reserved for herself in the pot of soup. I don't even know whether she's speaking plainly or in code."

"They're not telling you everything," his wife said.

"Of course. No married couple can ever tell everything, yet they want me to resolve what I don't understand."

"It's because you listen."

"My dear, it's good that someone does, otherwise who knows what can happen?"

In all these disputes, both the ones that were presented to Alhaji and the ones that were not, the quarreling spouses either reconciled or walked away with their lives. Except Beth. She had married a Nigerian entrepreneur and then decided after the first year that she didn't want to stay married to him. It was her husband's third marriage. The first had ended because, according to him, his wife became a registered nurse and began to make more money than him and to oppress him, as if she was now the man of the house. When he complained too much, the wife ended the marriage and kicked him out of the house. "Can you imagine that?" he still complained to anyone who would listen. "A whole me!" His second marriage ended because he believed his wife, whom he brought from Nigeria, was transformed the moment she became a member of the Nigerian women's meeting and began to listen to "assorted rubbish." How this sort of fellow met Beth and why she agreed to marry him were mysteries to me, although I was not altogether surprised. She was the sort of person who would see the glory of the sun even in a tunnel. But, this time, that ability failed her and she wanted to end the marriage.

"That man is a monster," she said to Ella. "What you see, and what I saw, is a human being; what I know now is a monster."

"Does he beat you?"

"No, he's too cunning for that, but I'm telling you I've seen his soul and it's as dark as a wintry night."

It didn't sound like Beth at all, more like a scene from an unfinished gothic film.

"I've never in my life heard Beth talk like that," Ella said. "She's always laughing."

"I know."

Ella encouraged her to quit the marriage. Her husband warned her that he would not allow any woman to "disgrace" him again. Beth moved out anyway and soon began another relationship. Her husband – or "former husband," as she called him – showed up one night in her boyfriend's apartment with a rifle, picked the lock, surprised the two in bed, and shot them to death. He was not satisfied even then. After they were already dead, he kept shooting at the naked bodies at will and swearing loudly until the police arrived. At first, it seemed as if he would surrender, but he apparently changed his mind and killed himself too.

It was the worst incident to happen in the Nigerian community since I arrived in Houston. And a feast for the Houston press. Of all the many reports and analyses of the killings, I was incensed by one in *The Houston Daily*, "The Yellow Shoes of Death," which focused on Beth's love for yellow shoes. The writer used her "happy shoes," as she described them, to pontificate about her childlike personality and what she called her "adulterous affair" that "courted death at the hands of a demented husband." I was so offended that I wrote a rejoinder, which was never published. The Nigerian community disowned Beth's husband and held an elaborate wake for Beth, then quite a number of people went from Houston to Cheyenne, Wyoming to attend her funeral. To know Beth was to love her. How on God's earth could this have happened? Was her husband indeed demented or mentally unstable or bipolar or tripolar or any of the other unnerving ways in which he was described? I had thought the fellow was a clown, not a killer. Was he like me, or I like him, in some sense? That thought did keep me awake at night.

Ella was crushed, and some of her fears about me bobbed to the surface for some time. She mourned Beth, her soul sister and only sibling, for a long time, sometimes crying every day, sometimes without tears. It was a very difficult period for us.

But death was not done with us. My father died about two years after Beth's murder. Ella and I had started planning our wedding, in a tentative sort of way, and that plan included traveling to Nigeria so that she could meet my father. Three years had passed since I finished my doctoral study and deviated from the family tradition by staying back in America. I had been home only once since then. My father had looked at me in extended silence then. "Listen, Ile," he finally said, "I'm happy you've found the love of your life. But you should still come home soon. This will be your mission one day."

Both of us knew what he was talking about – King Lazarus, my grandfather's legacy.

"But Uncle Ibe is here."

"I know, but it's you who has to continue the project."

"Why?"

"Because you're my son."

Unlike my uncle, my father was often as reticent as he was soft-spoken. I was almost on the verge of asking him for a clearer explanation, but I decided not to. My family seemed to love secrets, and it was not the first time I would feel that there was something not being said at all or not being said in a way that was comprehensible. One day, I sometimes told myself, these things would either be revealed or I would insist on clarity. But I kept postponing that day.

I was not surprised when Aunt Rosette called me that morning. She often called me from time to time, and she had even been to Houston once to see us. I was however surprised when she asked me, in a voice that sounded hoarse as if she had been crying, to speak with Uncle Ibe.

"Uncle Ibe is there?" As I asked the question, I wondered what sort of talk my aunt could not have with me but entrust to Uncle Ibe instead. It was one of those things about my family. My aunt always made it clear that she would not "be complicit in any kind of patriarchal condescension," but she still deferred to Uncle Ibe under certain circumstances.

"My son, death is a hawk," Uncle Ibe said as if he were continuing a conversation that we were already having before an interruption. His voice was unusually shaky, and it was not his custom to call me his son.

"What do you mean? What death?"

"The sharpening stone eats into the knife, just as the knife eats into the stone."

"What is it, Uncle Ibe? What stone, what knife? Where are you?" As I asked the questions, I wondered again if my uncle did not sometimes use proverbs just to sound a certain way rather than because of their meaning.

"You have to come home, Ile."

"What's going on? Is papa there too?"

"The deadliness of the python cannot be compared to the cunning of the tortoise, but how can even the tortoise go to war against a river that has swallowed an elephant?"

My uncle was very close to my father and had many stories to tell about their brotherliness when they were growing up. His death was one of the few things I know that deeply affected him.

My father "went to bed and did not wake up." It seemed an unusual way to die, without a story. "Oh, he was sick for a long time..." "My God, there was a crash and everyone died..." "No one lives forever; she died of old age..." Just "He went to bed and did not wake up." But the strangest part of the story was that my father had predicted the manner of his death. My mother had died the year before I left for Houston. She was knocked down by a car while crossing the road and was immediately taken to the hospital. But it was too late. She was declared dead on arrival. My mother was a housewife. She hardly went anywhere. Still, on one of the few occasions when she did, a car defied the odds and knocked her down. And she wasn't able to pick herself up like some other such victims I had seen. She died. I cried so much. Because my mother died. Because of the way my mother died. Because I had believed in a world that made sense, in the reasonableness of God. I cried so much that my father wiped his own tears and called me into a room. "You have to try and get a grip on yourself, Ile," he said to me almost in a whisper. "This is life; it's crying and laughing, and everything else, a whole lot of things, in between. Someday, when I go to sleep and not wake up, you shouldn't cry yourself to death too. It's a cycle that's been going on forever before us and a cycle that will go on forever after us. We cannot cry that the sky is blue or that the earth is brown. We just do what we can and try to be as happy as we can – against the odds. That's life." I was comforted more by the way he spoke to me than by his words, and I thought then that the image of him going to bed and not waking up was just a manner of speech. When he died in that manner, I hardly knew what to think. And it didn't matter that he himself had consoled me years before his passing. I still couldn't hold back my tears.

Joel and his wife, Sal or Salomé, organized a wake for my father in their home. It was a small gathering of friends and acquaintances who came together to wonder audibly about life and death over home-cooked meals and drinks. Sal was a petite brunette from Guadeloupe who often transited from English into Antillean Creole and back without a pause, but the meals that she prepared that night were mostly Antillean – accra, bokit, Colombo, rice, plantains, seafood. "Americans don't understand sorrow," she sometimes said. "This country is too rich and too big. But Guadeloupe, it's an island, small, poor, and you know what makes the sea flow? Our tears. It's true. Évwé!" Sal's tears often flowed freely.

That night, I talked about my father – how, like his father, he had closed his eyes and put a finger down on a map. Bogota. That was why he went to school in Colombia. My grandfather had done the same. London. He attended the University of London. And that was why I came to Houston. My family had a way of usually not planning the things that people often did and then sometimes planning the things that people didn't.

Ella had looked forward to meeting my father in person and did not want "to meet him through his funeral." So, I went home alone to attend my father's funeral. I was gone for a month before returning to Houston, against the protests of Uncle Ibe and Aunt Rosette. My aunt insisted that my return – "if at all" – had to be temporary; she would manage King Lazarus in the interim.

"You?" asked Uncle Ibe.

"Shut up," my aunt responded sharply. "You think because I let you act the man sometimes that you're the head of this family?"

"Which family? You're already married and gone."

"No. I'm married, so I have two families. I never left this one. I was born into it, and I'm the head now."

"Ah," Uncle Ibe sighed, vigorously shaking his head. "When a traveler encounters something strange on the way, he knows the end has come."

"Let it come. We end, and we start again. That's life. Gbala gbala felu oke obulu ala."

It was the only proverb I ever heard my aunt use, and it almost made my head spin. I didn't even know that she knew any proverb, not to talk of one in what sounded like ancestral Igbo. It brought a look of utmost wonderment with a tinge of perhaps fear to my uncle's face, the look that I would always remember whenever I thought about my father's funeral. I could understand his surprise. But there was something else on his face. Was it fear? Of what? Sadness? About what? Or cynicism that my aunt was metaphorically talking about a correlation between extremism and madness? "Too much of anything is bad." He didn't respond with words. He wiped his forehead as if he had suddenly broken into sweat and whistled. "Phew!"

My family wasn't crazy, but we were sometimes quite dramatic – and confusing.

That was how it happened that four years passed after our first meeting before Ella and I finally got married. We began to make preparations for the wedding about four months in advance. Like most things that we did, the preparations started before I realized that we were finally getting married. She saw a bridal gown that she couldn't stop thinking about and she ordered it online. Once it arrived and I exclaimed how beautiful it was we were already planning a wedding. I had proposed to her a long time ago.

The first time someone asked Ella how I proposed to her, I thought that we were about to set the rumor mill ablaze with stories of how "homemade" my proposal was.

"Oh, it was the most amazing sight," Ella said, smiling beautifully. "We were taking a ride round Galveston Bay, or so I thought. We were halfway across when the whole bay seemed to light up. Suddenly, we were literally in this circle of lights, and there was an orchestra that seemed to be playing in the water. Then a luminously white eagle draped with the American flag fluttered into the boat with an engagement ring..."

"For real?"

"For real."

"Oh, my God, that's the most beautiful proposal ever. How did he arrange all that?"

"It's a secret," I said and tried my best not to appear stunned.

"You mean Ile can be that romantic and resourceful? You're lucky, my dear. You've found a very special one."

I had to act as if I had heard the story before, as if I had in fact done all that, knowing that a surprised expression on my face would have ruined Ella's story.

"What's that all about?" I asked her afterward. "You mean you can make up a story like that on the spur of the moment?"

She laughed. "I should have been a poet," she said as if that answered the question.

"Seriously, Emmanuella..."

"Emmanuella? You only remember my full name when you're not happy about something. They wanted a story to whisper about. I gave them one to shout to the four winds. I should be taking a bow."

"You're something else."

"I know. That's why you wooed me like I was oxygen and you were gasping for breath."

"That was quite a performance, my dear. I almost had tears in my eyes."

"Thank you. That's more like it. Did you notice that Ioma wiped her eyes with a handkerchief? I didn't know she carried one. Don't mind these people. They're scouting for the next big gossip."

"But they're your friends."

"Sal, yes. And she knows the true story. Didn't you see how she was laughing as if she was at Comedy Central? The other ones are friends-with-caution. You and I know how you proposed, and I think it's the best proposal ever. But that's not what they want to hear."

The wedding went very well. Joel was my best man and Sal was Ella's maid of honor. My friendship with Joel had expanded to include dinners at home, his or mine, and that was how Ella and Sal became best friends. Ella always had "friends," but I used to tease her that her only friend was Beth. Although they appeared to be different kinds of people, Ella and Sal bonded easily. Ella was a bit mischievous, lovingly so; Sal had a more solemn personality. Ella hardly cooked; Sal could cook a ten-course meal alone. While she cooked she sang such uplifting hymns that Joel joked that he always got a "free trip to the Promised Land" along with the meal. Like Beth, Sal had a good heart, the sort of person who seemed to have no spite in her words and actions. "She's like Beth," Ella said. "If she asks you to lie down you can go to sleep without a care. I love her." Coming from Ella, those were no simple words. I had no more sense of guilt associating with Joel. There was no longer any need for me to sneak out. Ella often encouraged me to go because she had something planned with Sal anyway.

Uncle Ibe declined my invitation to attend the wedding in Houston with as many proverbs as he could muster. The only sense I could make of all of them together was that he did not like to fly.

"Flying is actually the safest way to travel," I said to him.

"That may be so, but who says I must travel? Do you think I would have ever left the village if not for my sister and the madness of Isaiah?"

"But flying..."

"Is the safest way to travel. You already said that. Ile, I'm happier on land."

"Kind of like you," Joel said when I told him the story. "Your uncle doesn't like to fly; you don't like to cruise."

"They're not the same thing."

"They're actually more similar than you think. To fly to Houston your uncle has to cross the Atlantic. To go on a cruise, you have to sail on water."

"Still, not the same thing."

"It's a loss anyway."

My aunt came, with her husband – a gangly fellow whose stiffness sometimes made him seem like a cardboard image with whiskers. He came to the wedding, spent another day and left. My aunt then settled down to explore and buy up the whole of Houston. She spent the day at exotic shopping malls and half the night touring and sampling the cuisine in upscale restaurants. She attended every Nigerian event she could, sometimes going from eating jollof rice and egusi soup to dining on Lobster à la Provençale. By the time she left, she had become so popular that people greeted her as an ambassador: "Ojemba!"

"America is sweet," she told me. "I'll come again. But that does not mean you shouldn't come home, the sooner the better."

For Ella and I, it was the best of times. Sometimes when I thought about our relationship I almost gasped. What would have happened if Idris had not got a job and left or if Ella had arrived one or two months later or if I had still gone ahead with my plans? I had stayed back in America because of Ella and it was the best decision I ever made in my life. But how could this beautiful thing have happened serendipitously? What did that say about the world? What if I had not gone to live in that particular apartment complex or that particular apartment? Was that why my grandfather had decided to simply close his eyes and put a finger on a map?

It was after the wedding that I decided to try and get a tenure-track job. I had not minded adjunct positions previously because I always thought that my stay in America would soon come to an end. I would convince Ella to move to Nigeria with me, and that would be that. She didn't need convincing. "As long as you'll be there with me," she told me. After my father's death, I knew I had to return home but I also felt that I was not quite ready yet.

When I did get the job, it was outside Texas – all the way over in Tennessee.

"So, we'll move to Tennessee," Ella said supportively.

"What about your job?"

"Well, you'll go and check things out first. I'll get another job and then I'll join you, probably next year."

"You seem to have it all worked out."

"My dear, this is not Houston marriage o. This is original Mbaino marriage." Her parents had left Mbaino years ago to settle in America. They had never been back home, so Ella knew Mbaino more as a name than a place.

"See your mouth," I teased her. "As if you know where Mbaino is."

We both laughed.

That was how I moved to Memphis, into an extended-stay hotel while I hunted for a house that would be a new home for us.

GALVESTON, September 15 – One week ago at this hour of the night the elements of earth and the powers of death were conspiring to bring about one of earth's greatest tragedies, and while that tragedy is now a part of the world's history, its fullest meaning, its direst peril, will never be pictured on the minds of any, save those who felt the chill blast of death, but through some inscrutable means of Providence did not fall as victims to its fury.

And it is better that the world does not know, that the world does not feel, what Galveston knows and feels. For, while all the world is sad, with Galveston, the city itself is the saddest spot on earth.

The woe, the misery, the suffering and the mighty march of death's angel have paralyzed the city by the sea for the time, and it is well that other cities were not so paralyzed, that they might bury the dead and minister unto the living.

I saw a friend to-day, a man who had fought against the wind and battled against the tide in Galveston. He lost a very dear sister and several cousins, but he was heedless of all this, and worked in the morgue, where scores of unshrouded dead were hastily prepared for their last long rest.

He strived to do this duty until he was ready to drop from exhaustion, but he did not cease his efforts for the welfare of his stricken people. He procured a pistol and went out to patrol the streets, to protect the living and guard the dead.

He saw a man, a white man, stoop to cut off a dead finger on which glistened a ring. A shot rang out and the ghoulish vandal was added to the numberless bodies that were swallowed up by the waves.

Speaking of the occurrence to me, my friend said:

"Until then I knew not what manner of man I was. I had always had a horror of bloodshed, but I shot that man with as little compunction as I would have smashed the head of a poisonous snake with a stake."

– The St. Louis Republic, *September 16, 1900*

"Your grandfather did what?" Ella asked when I called her from my hotel room that evening. "What are you talking about, Ile? Are you OK?"

"I'm fine. I still don't understand what's going on, but I got a voicemail from someone in South Africa saying he has a message for me from my grandfather."

"Is he a medium, a spiritualist?"

"I don't know. I think he's an attorney. I'll call him back on Monday. Meanwhile, I'll call Uncle Ibe and see what he has to say."

"Please, do, and call me back after that. I don't know what to think right now."

"I think there's been some sort of misunderstanding somewhere. I'll call you back."

I then called Uncle Ibe.

"Hallo," he answered.

I've suggested to my uncle a few times that there is no "a" in "Hello," and I'm sure he knows that, but that has not stopped him from answering almost every phone call with a "Hallo."

He listened to what I had to say. After I finished, I expected an outburst from him about "bogus people" and their "bogus" ways but he was uncharacteristically quiet.

"Hello, Uncle Ibe, are you still there?"

"I'm right here. Where else would I be?"

"I didn't hear anything from you."

"You say this fellow, William or Willem, is from where?"

"Stellenbosch, South Africa."

"And he said your grandfather is alive?"

"No, he said he has a message for me on behalf of my grandfather."

"What is the difference? Anyway, I'm sure he doesn't know what he's talking about. We buried Father a long long time ago, before you were born."

"You mean he died a long long time ago?"

"Isn't that what I said? You think we buried him alive?"

There was something about the conversation that was rather odd.

"Anyway, I'll call this Willem back on Monday and then I'll know what this is all about. I just wanted to talk to you first."

"You did well."

I was even more dissatisfied after speaking with Uncle Ibe, so I called my aunt. After I told her why I was calling she also fell quiet. Both my uncle and my aunt were never at a loss for words, so her response was as strange as my uncle's.

"Is there a problem, auntie? Did I say something wrong?"

"No, but you should talk to Ibe. He's the head of the family. I mean, he's also the head of the family."

I could hardly believe my ears. My aunt was deferring to my uncle without any argument? What was going on? What could possibly be going on? I was still contemplating what to do next when my phone rang. It was Uncle Ibe, the first time that he had ever called me since I moved to America.

"Hallo, is that Ile? You should come home," he said without any preamble.

"What's the matter, uncle? I'm sure you know that I live in America. I can't come home just like that."

"It doesn't matter if you live on the moon. You need to come home."

"Why?"

"We need to talk."

"We're talking, uncle."

"This is not phone talk. I know the world has changed, but some things still need to be discussed in person."

"What is it that we need to talk about in this case?"

"About your grandfather."

"What about him?"

"You need to come home. You should come with your wife if you can, otherwise just come, you hear?"

Whenever she was mad at my uncle, my aunt described him as "an imp" or "a rascal." I thought my uncle was too big to be an imp. But I had never doubted that, regardless of his playfulness, Uncle Ibe knew when to be serious and what to be serious about. I believed that he was being serious in his insistence that I should come home. But what did that mean? Someone calls me from the other side of Africa and leaves a nonsensical message and my uncle wants me to fly across the Atlantic Ocean to talk about it in person. What was going on?

"Did your grandfather have another family?" Ella asked when I told her about my conversation with Uncle Ibe.

"How did you get to that possibility?"

"Or is he... still...alive, in South Africa?"

"I asked Uncle Ibe the same question and he repeated that he died forty-four years ago. But there's clearly something he wants to say to me concerning my grandfather."

"Then you have to go to Nigeria. We have to go to Nigeria."

"We?"

"Yes, we. This must be important."

I also came to that conclusion when I finally got through to Willem on Monday. I had spent the whole weekend wrestling with the situation, sometimes like a blind man in an animal cage – afraid that I might stumble on something that would devour me. If my grandfather was still alive, what would that mean – that he was cast out by his family or that he turned his back on his family all these years? If he did, then what sort of man would that make him? And why would the entire village still celebrate him as if he were a god?

"You are Ile, I-l-e, right?" Willem asked after I introduced myself.

"Yes, I am."

"You need to come to South Africa, to Stellenbosch."

Suddenly, there were many distant places that I "had" to go to.

"Could you please tell me why you called me?"

"I've been searching for you for some time now. You're a difficult man to trace." It was as if he was somehow trying to feel me out with a preamble.

"OK, you've been searching for me," I said testily. "Why?"

"We are a law firm and we represent your grandfather, Mr. Ile Ka."

"Ileka!"

"No. Ile Ka."

"Then there must be an error," I said with relief. "My grandfather's name was Ileka."

"He changed it. I'll send you a picture to verify, but I'm sure he was your grandfather. He passed away a few months ago and bequeathed his estate to you."

"My grandfather passed away a few *months* ago? *My* grandfather? My grandfather died forty-four years ago, eleven years before I was born. I know his grave in my village. He never met me; I never met him."

"That is why you have to come to South Africa."

When I put down the phone, I suddenly had a headache. This was too much for me to wrap my head around. My past had seemed so perfect. My grandfather "came out of the forest" or "out of the night" and etched his name in glory. But history is often crispier than the truth.

After I looked at the picture that Willem emailed me, I knew I had to go to Nigeria and South Africa. I did not meet my grandfather alive, but there was so much talk about him and so many pictures of him that I would have recognized him anywhere. He was forty-four years old when he "died." If Willem's story was correct, then he had lived another forty-four years. Even in his old age, his facial features remained more or less the same – the same wide nose, high cheeks, the fire in his eyes that seemed inextinguishable, the same prizefighter's build, and the furrow across his forehead that the villagers said was the mark of the river. Did this mean that my grandfather had indeed lived forty-four years in South Africa after we thought that he was dead? And what "estate" was Willem talking about? My grandfather had left everything that he had to his children. Did he make another fortune? If he did, why would he leave that to me, whom he never met, instead of his children? It was still possible that all this could be a mix-up, I told myself but with less conviction than I had just a few days ago.

"You need to stop driving yourself crazy with all kinds of thoughts," Ella advised. "We'll deal with this the way it unfolds."

I agreed with her, but there was still the problem of how I would get a one-month leave at the beginning of a semester in order to travel to Nigeria and South Africa. I felt I needed that much time, but what would I tell my department chair? During my campus visit when I was interviewed for the job, we had gone out for dinner and one of the things that we talked about – of all the subjects in the world – was our grandfathers. I couldn't go now to tell him that, no, my grandfather never died or that he had now resurrected. And I couldn't imagine waiting four months, until the end of the semester, to solve this puzzle.

"I don't understand," Aaron, my chair, said when I broached the subject, looking penetratingly at me as he always did. Sometimes, he made me want to turn around and see what was behind me that he was looking at so intently through me. His glasses seemed oversized but, in my mind, they emphasized his acuity. "You told me your grandfather was dead. I remember because we talked about my grandfather too. What's going on?"

"I really don't know. My uncle still says my grandfather died forty-four years ago, but there's an attorney in South Africa that called me to say he only died four months ago and bequeathed his estate to me. That's why I've decided to travel to Nigeria and South Africa. It's important to me."

"It should be. I still remember some of the things you said about your grandfather. But it's the beginning of a new semester. If you speak to HR, you should get a week off to attend your grandfather's funeral, if there's going to be one. Other than that, you should wait until the end of the semester."

"That's four months away. I can't even concentrate. This South African attorney said they had to contact someone in Houston to go to my former school and ask about me. That's how they found me."

"They couldn't just google your name?"

"You remember I told you I legally changed my last name a few months ago. So, all their searches led to that college in Houston. But they couldn't get the information they wanted any other way than to send someone down there."

"That sounds serious, but it's still the beginning of the semester."

I had only been in the city about two and a half weeks and only one week in the school, but I was not wrong about Aaron. He was the sort of person who would help if he could, even if that sometimes meant unconventional solutions. I worked out a plan with him. I could take a month off if I could arrange make-up classes with my students before my departure and immediately after my return. I also had to prepare and upload my lectures for the entire semester online. It was a precaution, something the school had started asking all faculty members to do.

"You have to be back here in person after one month, no matter what happens. That's not negotiable."

"Of course." I could not thank him enough.

Fortunately, I was able to get my students to agree to make-up classes on Saturday and Sunday.

"Get ready," I told Ella on the phone. "I'm coming to Houston and then we're flying to the real Nigeria."

"You know I've been waiting for this my whole life."

Unlike some Nigerians born in America, Ella wanted to see and taste and feel Nigeria. Her Nigerianness, she felt, was somehow incomplete without the experience. But she could only travel for ten days because it was also the beginning of the semester for her and it wasn't her grandfather, as her chair pointed out to her.

At the beginning of the next week, a little more than one week after listening to Willem's message, Joel and Sal drove us to the airport to board our flight to Atlanta, then Lagos. "Take good care," Joel said as he shook hands, then embraced us individually. Sal called for a group hug and then bid us farewell, teary-eyed, in Antillean Creole. Good old Joel and Sal. Like aging wine, our friendship had become even better flavored with time.

The Book of Everything

2

The first thing Ella did when we left the airport terminal in Lagos was to bend down, pick up sand and sprinkle it on herself, drawing more attention to us. She had aroused a lot of curiosity since our arrival, receiving compliments for her beauty and kudos as a "returnee African American." Even the customs official who had first asked for a bribe in a roundabout fashion so that he would let us pass without searching our luggage, a favor I had not solicited, sort of changed his mind and said to me instead: "You do well, my brother. Your wife fine no be small, fine pass the kin' oyibo women wey our people dey carry come home."

"She's not oyibo," I told him. "She's Nigerian like me."

"She be Nigerian, eh, with that nose and American accent and American passport? OK, no problem, wey her Nigerian passport?"

"We didn't have enough time to get one, but..."

"OK, if you say so," he shrugged, like someone who did not really care or had indeed seen other Nigerians like her pass through the airport with American passports. He went back to asking for a bribe. "Nigerian o, American o, we dey here. Una suppose do us well."

"People look at you here as if they know you, or they just walk up to you and begin a conversation," Ella said after the customs official finally waved us through. "It's almost as if I'm at a Nigerian party in Houston."

"You see, you've had plenty of preparation."

"What's with all the vibe, the excitement all around? It's as if everything begins and ends as an exclamation."

"It's the way we are sometimes."

Seeing her sprinkling sand on herself made me wonder if that had anything to do with something she had seen or that I had said.

"What are you doing, Ella?"

"Following Sal's advice. Now, I'm a hundred percent

Nigerian."

"That Sal, she traveled all the way to Memphis without leaving Guadeloupe."

"They were made for each other, Sal and Joel."

Nathan was at the airport to pick us up. He was the childhood friend whose foot I had almost severed. We never stopped being friends because of the incident. We even went to the same college – Nathan in the Law department and myself in the English department – and were roommates while I was there. Growing up, we quarreled and made up and quarreled and made up in ways that cemented our lifelong friendship. Neither of us was perfect; neither of us cared for perfection. Every time people heard what I did to Nathan with a machete, they told him that he must be insane to still be talking to me. Nathan would smile and say something goofy. "But it was the machete that cut me, not Ile. So, why should I be mad at him?" "They don't understand," he would sometimes say to me afterward. "We were just crazy kids." After I was expelled from college, I often wondered if Nathan still believed that. No, he couldn't, because he witnessed the same sort of anger take over me and he practically saved me from becoming a murderer. Maybe he already realized that before the incident and that was why he brought those reinforced handcuffs along.

Nathan was not as big as I was, but he was almost as tall. His sinewy muscles testified to his devotion to athletic endeavors, running the sprint in elementary school, the short and the long races in high school, then both the short and the long races as well as martial arts in college. He did not look it, but Nathan was one of the strongest people I ever met. We used to joke back in elementary school that he walked as if he was ready to pounce. And he did pounce once in a while. On the occasions that our arguments devolved into fisticuffs, I always lost. Nathan had what we called "a single bone," which was our way of explaining the knockout blows that he was capable of unleashing effortlessly. Perhaps that was one reason I had despairingly resorted to the machete, some of the villagers had reasoned, but I knew that was not what happened. Something had taken over me so swiftly and completely that I had not been able to think at all. And that thing had apparently made me perhaps twice as strong during that period, otherwise how could I have cut so deep through Nathan's "single bone"?

My friendship with Nathan had defied distance. After college, he moved to Lagos to practice, and I stayed back in Fegge with my parents before going for a master's degree. Fegge was the riverside market town where my father, who was also a medical doctor, ran what used to be my grandfather's hospital and King Lazarus. But distance has a way of interfering anyway, like a traveler with his back against the wind who gathers dust nevertheless. We spoke over the phone and every time we met we dusted off any windy deposits on our friendship as if we had never parted. But both of us knew that over the years something intangible had changed between us. Whatever it was, we believed, it was unlikely to ever become greater than our bond. We were no longer friends; we had become brothers.

Nathan was very happy when I called him with news of our visit and wanted us to spend a night or two with him and his family before leaving Lagos. But I knew Nathan already had five children, so I talked him into recommending a nearby hotel instead. After we checked into the hotel, we went to his apartment to meet his family, especially "Agatha Swish Swish," the name we used to call her when we went to a coeducational school together. We thought then that she was so proud that even her skirt swished pridefully whenever she walked past. Nathan ran into her many years later, and she embraced him like an old friend. That was the beginning of a new kind of relationship between them. I had met her since then and we had become friends. I sometimes wondered whether it was simply the nature of things that we were so mean toward her as children. "I knew you were a troublemaker," she told me years later, "and he, Nate, was dying for me. That's why I swished my skirts so much. I no send." And we laughed. Nostalgia, the good old days, the god of memory – the greatest tonic on earth if well-distilled.

Agatha and Nathan had prepared a feast for us, enough food perhaps to feed a clan. Ella recognized many of the dishes, having seen them at Nigerian parties in Houston, but they were more delicious than she remembered. "Seems now that something was missing in the ones I ate back in the States," she said. We ate as much as we could, but there was still plenty of food left. We thanked Agatha profusely, but she insisted that Nathan did as much of the cooking as she did. We thanked both of them, then Nathan took us on a sightseeing tour of Lagos that ended up at a food market where almost everything was on sale – from cow tail pepper soup to roast bush pig. We savored the alluring aromas, but we could only order drinks. Agatha and Nathan had already overfed us. I joked that Ella looked at everything as if she had never seen them before and as if she might never see them again.

"Déjà vu. Everything is all new, yet I feel that I've seen them before. So, the Houston Nigeriana isn't fake after all – the accents, the dresses, the attitudes, the cuisine, everything."

"Not really, but it's a matter of scope and texture. Houston is like a copy of a Picasso painting. But this is the real thing, the one that Picasso painted when all his love affairs were in harmony."

"You!"

We had managed to find a corner where we could carry on some sort of conversation, sometimes with raised voices.

"What's this about your grandfather?" Nathan asked. Apparently, he was still trying to make sense of what I had told him over the phone.

"I don't know. I'm in a world right now in which everything is possible in a new kind of way. If that building suddenly begins to walk or this beer bottle to speak, I'll not be as surprised as my grandfather coming back to life after forty-four years."

"But the lawyer said he's dead again."

"Can you believe that? In none of the scenarios do I actually get to meet him. But maybe he'll come back to life again."

We laughed in a rather mirthless manner.

"Forty-four years is a lifetime for someone, especially a grandfather, to disappear without a trace. How does one return to life after that?"

"My grandfather was always a trailblazer."

We drank in silence for some time.

"I know Ile is your childhood friend," Ella said to Nathan, "but I want to thank you for looking after him for me."

"What are you talking about?" Nathan asked, a bit suspiciously.

"He told me about *the* incident, the incident*s*."

Nathan looked at me. "You told her?" He turned to Ella and waved his hand in the air. "Don't mind him..."

"I understand, Nathan, but we have to face it. It's a real thing."

Nathan looked at me again, more meditatively. "You've always been lucky, Ile. I think you're very lucky to find a woman like her."

I couldn't agree more.

Right from the beginning, Ella and I had promised to tell each other everything, but that was one story, the second incident involving Nathan, that I hadn't been able to tell her. I would have if she had asked specifically, but the first time she actually heard the details was at an anger management class.

It was my turn to tell my story.

"Hello, everyone, my name is Ile, and I have an anger problem. When I was nineteen years old, I almost killed a woman..."

I could see Ella sit up where she was. She knew there was

a second incident, but for some reason she had not asked me for details. I hoped she would still be there after I finished.

It was my second year in college. I was an only child, and maybe that was why my parents gave me more money than I needed. But I didn't party like the rich boys on campus. I bought fine clothes and gadgets, drove a car, and ate in expensive restaurants near campus. And it was in one of them that I met J. That was what she called herself. Even though some of the girls in our class had invited me out or sent me notes, it was J that I wanted. I couldn't stop thinking about her. Everything that she did, even the wrong answers she gave in class, fascinated me. She was too sophisticated to be ordinary. She was three years older than me and had been sent back to Nigeria by her parents because she always got into trouble "back home" in Oakland, California. There were two of them in our class. The other one, a hefty fellow who was about J's age, had been sent back to Nigeria by his parents in Dublin, Ireland. We called him Big Tony, and he was possibly the heftiest person on campus. Both of them were friendly toward each other, but we expected that. Big Tony was a truant, so we hardly saw him or the two of them together.

Anyway, I went to the most expensive restaurant near campus one day and found J sitting there looking discomposed. She did not have that superior air of someone who had lived in America and now had to live among barbarians like us. Instead, she was moping into space as if she was lost in time. I hesitated, then I went over to find out what the matter was. She said sharply that she didn't "want to be disturbed," so I left her alone. But I learned from the chatty waitress that her boyfriend had stood her up again and the restaurant was not willing to accept anything other than cash as payment for her bill. I was surprised that any man could treat her in that shoddy fashion, even more so that she could not settle a bill in a local currency such as the naira. I paid her bill. When she found out that she was free to go, she stormed out without as much as a look in my direction. I loved her more. She had style.

She must have reconsidered her behavior, I thought, because she began to sit next to me in class and somehow we started talking – and going out to restaurants and shopping together. I always paid the bill. Sometimes, she asked me for a loan. I was happy to oblige. She never paid back. No problem. What was money between friends? At my urging, she invited me to her room – an expanded space that could have been two or three separate rooms – and introduced me to her roommates. But it was a bland sort of introduction. "Hello, girls, this is Ile." And that was that. She didn't disclose what we were to each other or tell me the names of her roommates. No problem. I assumed that we were in a relationship nevertheless.

"I can see through her," Nathan told me. "She's along for the ride, not the destination."

"You're too old for a young man," I retorted. "She's really nice. You just need to get to know her better."

"Good luck, Romeo."

"Goodbye, Plato."

I was as happy as a lullaby. The only wrinkle in our relationship was that I could only kiss her, nothing more. Whenever I tried to do more than kiss her, she would kiss me more and tell me not to be in a rush. "You're not going anywhere. I'm not going anywhere. What's the rush?" Of course, I was not going anywhere. Who else would I want to be with other than J?

One weekend, she told me she had to travel all the way to Lagos to meet her parents who were visiting. She would be gone the whole weekend. I drove her to the taxi station, paid for a chartered taxi, and bid her farewell. "See you soon. I can't wait." The next day, as I walked back to my hostel, I ran into one of her roommates in a different part of the campus. She greeted me in a manner that was neither friendly nor hostile and added "See you later." It was the kind of expression that could mean something or nothing, depending. I kept wondering: Why on earth would she expect to see me later? Later that day or later in life or later what? Was J already back from Lagos? Did something happen? Was she being polite or sarcastic? I decided I was overthinking three simple words. When I mentioned the encounter to Nathan, however, he told me in that way he had that something was afoot and insisted that we visit J.

"If she's not there, then she's not there. You just stopped by because you haven't heard from her. Or have you?"

I let him persuade me, and we walked in on J having a well-attended birthday party in her room, a party I had possibly paid for with a recent loan. Big Tony was there. J was sitting on his lap, and he was fondling her breasts as if they were alone. They were both giggling like new lovers experimenting with a new kind of laughter. She glared at me when she saw me as if I was something that belonged in darkness but had unaccountably been unearthed by light. According to Nathan, something he did not want to ever see again happened to me and I went berserk. I would have torn her to shreds if not for the combined intervention of himself and Big Tony, each of whom was stronger than me in normal times. When I recovered from my madness, the room was in shambles and I was in the reinforced handcuffs that Nathan had brought along. The police had already been called.

I spent a week in detention. J never showed up to press charges against me, but that did not stop the police or my cellmates from turning me into a kind of sport. They took turns castigating me, sometimes with severe blows to drive home their rhetorical attacks.

"Yeye man, woman no want you na im you wan' kill am. Na by force?"

"No mind am. Why you no go fight with your mates? Come fight me make I comot all the teeth for your mouth, you idiot of no nation."

"See im head. You dey form madness, abi? Imbecile!"

After my release, I found out that I had been expelled. The school administration did not interview me. They relied on the testimonies of witnesses and the anger of several students, who threatened to shut down the school if I was not severely punished. I tried to seek out J to apologize, but her roommates did not know where she was. I packed my things quietly and left. Nathan thought I should complain that the punishment was too severe. I preferred not to, but instead transferred to another college.

My parents were outraged by my behavior. After my father had scolded me for days and even threatened to disown me, he took me to see different psychiatrists, then a neurologist. The first psychiatrist "explored" with me any repression issues that I might have.

"What's the nature of your relationship with women?" she asked me.

"It's fine. Nothing unusual."

"Have you had any other girlfriend, I mean gone out with any other girl?"

"Yes, last year."

"Tell me more. What happened?"

"She transferred out of the school, otherwise we didn't have any problems."

"Do you miss her?"

"Sometimes, but I'd rather be with J, or so I thought."

"Why?"

"I don't know how to explain it. She makes my heart joyful."

"That's a vivid image. Do you think she feels the same way about you?"

"I know now that she doesn't."

"What made you think that she did?"

"We were together a lot, and we sometimes kissed and

promised each other the future. Everyone I know thought she was my girlfriend."

"Why were you so mad that day, because she didn't invite you to her party?"

"I'm not sure. I went in there and she was sitting on another man's lap and he was fondling her breasts and they were laughing gleefully."

"You were jealous?"

"I think so, but that's not why I lost it. Well, that probably had something to do with it. But I was mastered by a force beyond me."

"Has this happened before?"

"Yes, when I was nine years old I almost cut off my best friend's foot with a machete. We were arguing about whose mother was the better cook."

"You were talking..."

"Then he laughed at the idea of my mother being as good a cook as his. I lost it."

"Where did you get the machete?"

"I rushed out to get a stone or stick. I saw the machete lying around."

"And you decided to cut him?"

"I didn't know what I was going to do. I thought he would run away, but he showed no fear. He thought I was only trying to scare him. He even stuck out his foot and dared me to cut him."

"And you decided to do so?"

"I wasn't going to cut him. I told him to go and find someone else to kill him or, better still, to go back home so that his mother would cut his foot and cook it for him to eat. I put down the machete. They say I suddenly changed as I straightened up as if something had come over me, then I bent down and grabbed the machete. He must have known that something was wrong because he began to run away. I chased him, knocked him down, and almost cut off his foot."

"What happened next?"

"I think the action and the spurting blood and his screams brought me back to my senses."

The session went on and on, back and forth. After two sessions, she told my father that she didn't think I had cognitive problems or that I was "mad." The other psychiatrists that I saw arrived at dimmer conclusions, but they also didn't think that I was mad. My father seemed to think so and was apparently searching for a psychiatrist to confirm his suspicion. Eventually, he took me to see a neurologist.

The neurologist was very interested in my symptoms, the things I heard or saw before or during an attack – the sound of a train whistle, the thundering waves, and the changing patterns.

"These patterns, what are they?"

"Abstract designs or shapes."

"Squares, circles, what shapes?"

"It's a mix – squares that become circles, polygons that become triangles, all sorts of things."

"How long before the change from one form to another?"

"A second or less."

"Do they make you dizzy?"

"Sort of."

"What's the direction of the movement – east to west, north to south?"

"Everything happens very fast, and the movement doesn't happen according to a particular rhythm."

"Can you describe it?"

"Not sure."

"Can you work with a visual artist to recreate the pattern?"

"I wish I could. Everything happens swiftly and without consistency."

"What's the nature of the transition?"

"I don't understand."

"I mean, how does one form change into another? Does one form give way to another or does one become the other, that sort of thing?"

"It seems one dissolves into another, but these patterns are so active that they appear to make all manner of transitions."

"What about distance? Do they maintain the same virtual distance from you?"

"More or less, but there's really no distance. They seem to be right in front of me."

"Can you touch them, or rather do you feel as if you can touch them?"

"I've never tried; they seem more virtual than substantial."

"Colors, do they have colors?"

"Like the colors of a certain kind of moon dream. I don't think we have those colors in real life. I can't describe them."

"Do the colors change?"

"Yes."

"Size, what sizes are these patterns?"

"Not big, sometimes even tiny."

"Like showers?"

"Yes, and also a bit bigger. I think the dynamism of these patterns is difficult to describe. There's simply too much going on within a very short time."

Of all the symptoms, he was particularly interested in the changing patterns, but I couldn't describe them the way he wanted.

"What's the interval between the sound of the train whistle and the thundering waves and the changing patterns?"

"Seconds, I think. Everything actually seems to happen at once."

"At what point do you begin to lose control?

"I wish I knew."

After a long session, he ordered a brain scan. He concluded that there was nothing medically wrong with me in relation to my father's complaint. People then advised my father to take me to a dibia or a "miracle church" for spiritual healing. My mother urged him not to do so, and he did not.

It was not the very worst story that I ever heard at an anger management class, but I thought that people sort of looked at me differently after my confession. Ella was mortified, but she didn't walk away.

"I hope there's no other incident," she told me gravely, "because I can't take any more."

"None," I assured her. "And there won't be."

"There better not be. I'm not that strong."

"You?"

"I'm not as strong as you think."

I wanted to say something but thought better of it.

"You owe your friend so much," she said. "You nearly cut off his foot, and he still stayed around to save you from committing a murder."

"I do. That's why I sometimes disagree with the Kant that Joel quotes. The timber of humanity is not all crooked."

"I'll thank him specially whenever I meet him."

"Kant?"

"You're joking, eh? Of course not Kant. I mean Nathan."

Nathan accepted her thanks, but told her that we were brothers, so he only did what he ought to.

The next day, he drove us to the bus station for the journey to Isiani, my village. Uncle Ibe had told me there was no need for us to come to Abuja.

"This is not city talk. I will be – no, we will be – waiting for you in the village."

"Aunt Rosette too?"

"She says she's the head of the family, so that makes me the body, I suppose. If the body is there, the head has to be there too, otherwise there'll be bloody confusion."

I could imagine him chuckling.

Ella called for a group hug at the bus station and thanked Agatha and Nathan again for their hospitality. "Nothing do you," she added before we boarded a vehicle, an expression that could almost mean whatever needed to be said – "You're OK" or "I like you" or "You can do it" or "Thanks." Of all the many intriguing expressions she had heard in Lagos in just one day and one night, that was the one that she liked most.

We arrived in the village late in the afternoon. My grandfather had built a sprawling house, the largest in our village. It was so big that it was more like four houses attached to a central building. When I was young, we used to refer to it as Five Villa. It was completed in 1965, the year Uncle Ibe was born. No one knew why a man who had only three children would build such a huge house, but it was sometimes said that my grandfather intended all his offspring to live together in that mansion. After he died and my father inherited the house as the first son, he persuaded Uncle Ibe that he had the same right of inheritance to the mansion, so each of them lived in one part of it. Aunt Rosette claimed one part whenever she stayed over in the village. There was still an unclaimed part, but I preferred to stay in the part of the house that my parents had occupied.

The first thing I did when we arrived was to go and look at my grandfather's grave in a corner of the compound. It was still there. He was born in 1930 and died in 1974, the gravestone proclaimed. Nothing had changed.

"You have just arrived from a long journey," Uncle Ibe said, observing me. "We have not even greeted each other well. You have not even introduced your wife well. This is no time to be looking at old graves."

I was always happy to see Uncle Ibe and Aunt Rosette and we spent some time inquiring after each other and making Ella welcome. Both of them had left their families in Abuja to come and meet me in the village. Her only daughter lived in France. Many Nigerian students preferred to go to school in Anglophone countries because of the language or, recently, in China, which I was told was recruiting students from Africa. But Julia, Aunt Rosette's daughter, had been in love with everything French since she was taught the French language by a French woman in high school. French was not simply a language to her; it was "the language of high culture." She studied French in college and then decided to go to graduate school in Paris and then to work there as an editor. She had fallen in love with the city. I sometimes spoke with her on the phone, and she often had fascinating stories to tell about Paris. Sometimes, though, she did not have a happy story to tell. But, happy or sad, she always had a story. "You should write," I told her. "Who told you I'm not already writing?" she asked. I wasn't surprised.

Uncle Ibe had married a woman he met when he briefly worked in an office before he decided that he wasn't "an office person." My aunt sometimes teased him that she helped him get a good job but all he did was romance one of his colleagues and then run away. But while Ibe was not an office person, his wife, Udoka, was devoted to her office career. She was also a born-again Christian, unlike Uncle Ibe. Their differences seemed more obvious to other people than to the couple, and Ibe often told people: "Love has no other culture. It's not something for the village elders or the supreme pastor to decide; the heart decides." Many people advised him in the beginning that what he was contemplating was a recipe for disaster. He nodded as if he understood what they were saying but went right ahead with his marriage plan.

Despite the predictions of the naysayers, and there were many of them, he lived in peace with his wife and they had four children, two girls and two boys. To anyone who cared to listen, Ibe described himself as an active father and husband. But many people were uncertain that Ibe could be trusted as a marriage counselor and mocked his advice to "only marry someone who understands you and who you understand too." They muttered that he had a "rascal's luck," the same luck that often made him do well in enterprises that others had attempted and failed. "Luck?" Ibe asked rhetorically, disregarding the description of him as a rascal. "You see how our people are? When Ibe does well, it is luck but when they do well it is intelligence plus diligence. Ibe is this, Ibe is that. What has this Ibe done?"

But he was not in that sort of mood when he welcomed Ella and I to the village. "You are indeed like your grandfather," he said to me. "You went to America and you brought home the queen. In the old days, we would have initiated you into ogba ngbada."

"Be serious!" Aunt Rosette told him.

"I've always been serious. It's not my fault that the world doesn't always know it."

"I like him," Ella whispered to me. "He's real." She had said the same thing about Aunt Rosette, but I was not sure they were both "real" in the same sense.

"What was your grandfather?" she asked me. "An emperor? How did he build this sort of mansion?"

"He was a legend, you know that. The rest, that's why we came."

Ella insisted on seeing what she could of the village that evening, so I took her around, stopping at a few houses to greet old friends and relatives. The village was changing. There were newer houses, new kinds of restaurants, a bigger Catholic church, and other signs of modernity. But these were more like sprinkles, a few sprinkles, rather than frosting. The village was changing slowly, so it was still the sort of place where a piercing cry in the middle of the night could echo through the forest and send everyone scrambling to the source. People still drank river water and farmed long hours as if the earth was ever more reluctant to yield its bounties. But it was not uncommon even in this environment to hear the mention of "CNN" or "Chelsea, Arsenal, Man U" that suggested the presence of another world that was not yet fully formed.

"This is a different Nigeria," Ella said.

"From the one you saw in Houston?"

"Yes. Just when I had almost concluded that the Houston Nigeriana wasn't fake."

"It's not fake, but you can't see all of Nigeria from Houston."

"This looks like the sort of place where the 'African art' that made Picasso famous came from."

"You! What's your new fascination with Picasso?"

"We're in Africa."

Despite its village ambience, there was a bustling Jesus Jesus Church opposite the magisterial Catholic Church. By the time Pastor Isaiah died, his ministry had grown so much that it continued to thrive after him. Pastor Joshua, his successor, was careful, however, about the type of battles that he picked outside the church. The Catholic Church still had its loyalists, those who believed that it was the one true religion. But it seemed there were also many people who not only wanted salvation but required salvation and riches urgently. My uncle called them the "Today Today people" because of the song they often sang with passionate insistence:

> Today today
> Jesus will answer me
> Today today

"It's as if they're lying in ambush," Uncle Ibe would say. "I pity Jesus if He doesn't answer them today today."

"Be careful, Ibe," Aunt Rosette would caution. "You're practically begging to go to hell. I can't help you then."

"You too?"

"Yes, me. I don't joke about God."

"I wasn't joking," he said with a smile.

At the time he arrived, not even Uncle Ibe realized what sort of upheaval Pastor Isaiah's mission would cause in the area. No one appeared to know where he came from, so there were all types of speculations. He neither confirmed nor denied any of them, so the mystery deepened. Had he indeed worked with the idiosyncratic Pastor White in Fegge? Had he traveled all the way from Abuja or Lagos to minister to "forest villages?" Had he recently returned from America's Bible Belt full of Christian fervor? All these speculations gave way to a common narrative after the pastor passed. Some of his church members stepped forward to more or less tell the same story about him. If they were to be believed, Pastor Isaiah had only walked about twenty miles from Fegge to begin his church. Until that trek, he had worked as one of Pastor White's assistants. He had not left of his own volition but had been excommunicated because of his predilection for stepping forward during the healing sessions.

Pastor White had made it clear to his assistants that they were up there on the dais to assist him, nothing more. "An assistant assists, nothing else!" They could catch people recently touched by him as they fell down because his touch had imbued them with the Holy Spirit. They could chant or sing or "speak in tongues" as he made the blind see or the lame walk or the deaf hear. They could sing or shout "Hallelujah" or "O glory," but they couldn't step forward to take part in the healing of the afflicted because the Lord spoke and acted through him – only him. Every other assistant appeared to understand these instructions except Isaiah. From time to time, he would be possessed by what Pastor White called "a contrary spirit" and he would step forward, stand abreast with

Pastor White and lay his "contrary hands" on people waiting for Pastor White to heal them. And his touch seemed to cause some of these people to be so filled with the Holy Spirit that they trembled and fell.

Pastor White invited Isaiah to his office and calmly asked him. "What are you doing, Isaiah?"

Isaiah looked around him as if to indicate that he was only sitting down in front of the pastor, nothing more.

"Cut out the act," Pastor White hissed. "I don't mean what you're doing now. You know what I'm talking about. I mean what are you doing stepping up to lay your contrary hands on people who have come to me for healing?"

"I was only trying to assist..."

"Who asked you to assist in that manner? How can you, who is possessed by a contrary spirit, assist the Lord's anointed in healing the sick?"

"I am possessed by a contrary spirit? I don't understand, pastor."

"You came to me from who knows where. You said you had been called to enter my ministry to prepare for yours. I took one look at you and I knew you were a troublemaker. Despite that, I took you in. I knew you were kicked out of high school because you were dull and disobedient. Despite that, I took you in. I knew you were rusticated from the university because you were dull and defiant. Despite that, I took you in. I am telling you today to stop being contrary in my church, otherwise I'll throw you out."

Pastor Isaiah was surprised. How had Pastor White found out so much about him? He had never given any indication that he knew anything about him other than what he did in church. If he knew so much, why had he indeed taken him in?

The meeting apparently had an effect on Isaiah. He stopped stepping forward when he should only be assisting as instructed. People began to say that a meeting in Pastor White's office was guaranteed to heal even the devil. But Isaiah was not actually healed. A few months later, as Pastor White began to heal several people at once, instead of going from one to the other, Isaiah was carried away by the rousing excitement all around him. He broke into a different song than the rest of the congregation:

> What a mighty God we serve
> What a mighty God we serve
> Angels bow before him
> Heaven and earth adore him
> What a mighty God we serve

A surprised Pastor White gave him a withering look that was supposed to shut him up, but Isaiah's voice seemed to climb up a notch instead. "Get thou behind me, Isaiah!" Pastor White ordered. Isaiah's voice climbed up another notch. Pastor White turned his full attention to his unruly assistant. "Get thou behind me, Satan!" he ordered as he began to cast out the devil that he was certain had possessed Isaiah. But the devil in Isaiah, if indeed it was so, was by now bellowing so much that Pastor White recognized that extraordinary measures were needed. He signaled to his security guards. They stepped forward, tackled an otherwise uncontrollable Isaiah to the floor, bound his hands, and carried him out. Even then, everyone could hear his voice impossibly climbing another notch until he was apparently gagged.

Pastor White made it clear that "light and darkness have no relationship," so he would not "work with the devil." That was the end of Isaiah's apprenticeship under Pastor White, but he was not crestfallen. He took to the streets, in a fashion not dissimilar to the methods that Pastor White himself had used to build up his own following. But he had underestimated how powerful Pastor White had become and the effect of the constant reference he made to Isaiah as "the roaming devil." It did not take Isaiah too long to realize that he had to go somewhere else to build up his ministry. One day, he promised himself, he would return to Fegge and he would then show Pastor White who indeed was the devil between them. So, he began his trek away from Fegge, searching for another town, even a small one, to begin the Jesus Jesus Church. The name had come to him in a fit of inspiration. "The greatest name in the world is Jesus," he told his congregation, "and the more we chant that name the stronger its effect is. Come on, repeat it, treble it." He ultimately concluded that "Jesus Jesus Church" served his purpose better than "Jesus Jesus Jesus Church."

It did not take Pastor Isaiah too long to decide that one way to root his own ministry was to root out all "contrary" ones. It did not matter that he had already succeeded in building a fairly strong church through the power of healing that he professed and exhibited. He still felt the need for what he considered bold statements. But when he derided the Catholic Church, he was a bit surprised by the mixed response. Many of his converts had recently been Catholics. No one said anything explicitly to Pastor Isaiah, but he had become better at listening and hearing the unsaid since his excommunication by Pastor White. So, he decided that there was a less ambiguous battle that he could fight and win. Why not wipe out the "pagan shrines" that still distracted some of his congregants, implanting a contrary spirit within them? Better still, why not speak the word and see it transformed into deed? What happened next was in his eyes a small measure of the inestimable power of God. He had hardly finished talking about ending the blight of "demonic shrines" with the power of God when young men began stepping up asking him to send them to do the deed. He knew then that he had indeed come a long way and that the time for his triumphal return to Fegge was at hand.

Pastor Isaiah was particularly happy that he had managed to stay away from scandal during his rise. He had his spies, so he knew that people whispered all sorts of things about him – that he himself visited pagan shrines in faraway riverside towns, that he loved widows and in fact all manner of women in his "twilight bedrooms," that he starved his church of funds but blessed himself with the tithes of his congregants, that he staged "healings" and "testimonies." But no one had been able to prove these allegations or even voice them out in a way that mattered. In his heart, he thanked Pastor White for teaching him, perhaps without really meaning to, how to grow a church with the kind of methods that people normally ascribed to magicians. He looked forward to confronting him soon to see who had fared better between them.

But that confrontation never happened. Instead, Pastor Isaiah died mysteriously. First, there was bewilderment, then people began to murmur that maybe the old gods had not quite died, at least not in the way that Pastor Isaiah had announced. But these murmurs were quickly stifled when the church elders came together and decried them as blasphemy and assured anyone uttering such heresy of "perpetual hellfire." My uncle scoffed. "That's a new one," he said. "I thought hellfire was perpetual anyway. I didn't know that the Today Today people have different sorts of hellfire. You can lease one corner for one week and see how hot it really is before deciding whether to go for the lifetime corner or to get the hell out of there." Many of the villagers ignored him, although a few of his former colleagues in the ogba ngbada brotherhood asked him to return to the land of the dead where he belonged and create more space for the living. "I didn't know I was taking up all the free space available," he fired back. "I'm on my way home. You can have the space I just quit – for free."

After the Jesus Jesus Church buried and mourned Pastor Isaiah, it was torn apart by a power tussle. Like Pastor White, Isaiah had several assistants, but he had also made it clear that he was the supreme leader. Everybody else did what they were told. He had a committee of church elders, but these were not pastors and their role was mostly advisory – when he cared to consult them. More often than not, he consulted only God in Heaven before he did as he pleased. So, after he died, the church was leaderless. Some people predicted that some ambitious assistants would leave then to begin their own ministries, but no one did so. The Jesus Jesus

Church had grown quite rich both in cash and other kinds of capital.

Soon, one of the assistants, Pastor Philip, proclaimed himself the new head of the church because he had been the last person that Pastor Isaiah spoke to before he died. Some people queried this story and even suggested that he might know a thing or two about the true story of the pastor's demise. But Philip wasn't the sort of person to succumb to what he described as "idle and ungodly threats." He was better educated than Pastor Isaiah and spoke as if he were God's secretary with a confidential knowledge of His private notebooks. He was a short man who favored a well-groomed beard that his opponents described as "ungodly." Philip laughed at them, pointing out that the God he worshiped looked only into the spirit. "People who focus on the person had better think again about the kind of God they worship," he said. In his mind, no other assistant could stand up to him and he was certain that his ordination as Pastor Isaiah's successor was only a matter of time.

But he met his match in Pastor Joshua, who proclaimed himself a spiritual successor to the Joshua that led the children of Israel to the Promised Land. He was the "new Isaiah," he announced. "I am not suggesting anything negative about our pastor, who is now in heaven," he pointed out, "but it is time to renew the old covenant – in the same way as the New Testament came after the old one. I am the Risen Isaiah." Philip was welcome to claim that he was the last person to see Pastor Isaiah before he died. He, Joshua, saw the holy pastor "in the spirit, after his death." Joshua was only a bit taller than Philip, but he was of medium build, which made him seem taller. Instead of a beard, he was always clean-shaven and preferred "livelier" suits in bright colors to the somber colors that Philip favored.

The church elders found themselves in the middle of a battle they did not initially realize had already started. They called a meeting to decide on the way forward, but it soon turned into a shouting match between the supporters of the two opponents. Another attempted meeting abruptly ended with someone's front tooth being knocked out when the shouting transformed into punching. Having proven they were unable to resolve the crisis, some of the elders released a statement that they would wait for inspiration because they were certain that God would never desert his people. The church members were similarly divided, which made everything difficult. When Philip tried to hold a church service, Joshua's supporters shouted him off the dais, calling him a "fill up" who was only interested in personal aggrandizement. His supporters did the same thing to Pastor Joshua calling him a "Josh not" who judged everyone as if he were God – even though the Bible had counseled: "Judge not, and ye shall not be judged."

The more vigorous among the church elders managed to restore some sort of order. While they were waiting for "spiritual direction," they insisted that the two contenders hold different services. Philip and his "Original Jesus Jesus Church" met in the mornings; Joshua and his "Reformed Jesus Jesus Church" met in the afternoons. Initially, the membership of both groups appeared even. But the crossovers soon began with people leaving one group to go to the other for all sorts of personal and "spiritual" reasons. Sometimes, they returned to their original group, having satisfied themselves that they made the right decision in the first place; sometimes, they did not. After a few months, it was obvious that one group had grown populous, much more so, than the other. People said Philip was an inspiring preacher who spoke of heaven as if it was indeed his home but that Joshua was a better healer who performed "signs and wonders" in the name of the Lord. And apparently it was the signs and wonders that counted most. Joshua's Reformed Jesus Jesus Church had almost doubled in size. The same vigorous church elders who had restored order now boldly denied Philip and his small group access to the church premises. Pastor Isaiah's Jesus Jesus Church had become Pastor Joshua's Reformed Jesus Jesus Church, and that was the group that held sway – opposite the Catholic Church – in Isiani.

Pastor Joshua strengthened his hand by traveling outside his headquarters to village churches to hold revivals or "power conferences." Pastor Isaiah never traveled outside his headquarters, so this was a new phenomenon that made church members very excited as they prepared for what they called the "Holy Coming." Some people whispered that Pastor Joshua's itinerancy was a sign of panic because he knew that Pastor Philip had not gone too far away to continue his ministry with the intention of one day returning to reclaim the Jesus Jesus Church. Followers of Pastor Joshua described that sort of talk as "daydreaming" or "a symptom of terminal malaria." The village churches to be visited ignored such "nonsense talk" and upped their preparations to receive the "Holy Joshua" in their midst. In Isiani, the countdown – and frenetic preparations – had begun when we arrived. It did not matter that Pastor Joshua's visit was still more than one month away.

"You don't know the half of it," Uncle Ibe told us. "People are learning new dances, maybe even new walks, thinking up new hairstyles, designing new clothes, probably dreaming new visions. It's almost as if Christ himself is on his way to our small village. Unbelievable."

"Leave them alone," my aunt protested. "Pastor Isaiah was a lunatic, but whatever his followers are doing they're doing in the service of God."

"Are you sure these people are not simply afraid?"

"Afraid of what, and who are you to judge?"

"Of course," said my uncle. "Who am I to judge?" I wasn't sure if he was simply being Uncle Ibe.

Perhaps the conflicts and euphoria of religion in my village had to do with true belief. Or perhaps it had to do with a creeping fear of death. My village was in the region of the country that was being ravaged by erosion. Some of the villagers said that it was because Pastor Isaiah destroyed the shrine of the earth goddess that the earth was eating itself. Some of the Reformed Jesus Jesus Church faithfuls described the signs of erosion as "the fingers of God" or "the judgment of God," depending on their inclination. But it did not seem as if the signs were indeed searching out only sinners or sparing only saints. Others pointed out that the scourge was even worse in places where no shrine had been destroyed. Some others explained that the earth was being moved from one place to the other by other forces. As the movement continued, parts of the village began to seem rather unsteady, like a drunk with wobbly legs but who was still standing. One of the villages nearby woke up one morning and this movement of the earth from one place to another had transformed into a landslide. Houses disappeared into the depths of the earth as if they were architectural models now carelessly disposed of in open sewers. The tragedy was unnerving. Alarm bells of fear and frustration went off in the surrounding villages, including ours. The Reformed Jesus Jesus Church organized a seven-day fast "to seek the face of God." Government officials arrived from the capital in Lagos suits or Abuja robes with serious faces, made staccato speeches, took selfies, and retired with happy faces. "Bogus people," Uncle Ibe scoffed. Aunt Rosette assured everyone that she would move mountains to see that the problem was solved. So far, whatever mountains she had in mind remained rooted where they were.

"It's a troubled country ruled by idiots with diseased brains," she said.

I showed Ella as much of the village as I could that evening and the next day, both its aspirations and its scars. By the second day, however, both of us were impatient to sit down with Uncle Ibe and Aunt Rosette and unravel the mystery that had brought us all that way. Uncle Ibe was unsure whether Ella should join us for the meeting, but Aunt Rosette overruled his doubts.

"She's one of us now, no less."

"I wasn't saying any less, but this is a delicate matter."

"Delicate or not, this is now her family. Aren't you the same person who asked them to come together? And rightly so."

Ubelegede k'ana ekene eze muo.

"You greet the king of the spirits in a certain way," Uncle Ibe began.
"Ibe, can we cut out the proverbs?" asked Rosette.
"Uncle..."
"Listen to me," Uncle Ibe said solemnly. "And listen well. This is not a story to hurry over. I've been pondering some of these things for a long time. I know the world has changed. As Father used to say, the world is always changing. To tell you this story, I have to go back to a world that no longer exists, a world that I loved, a world that I still love. But I'm now an Afro Christian, which means I've accepted the new order, some of it, but I've not rejected the old one, some of it too. I never knew that would happen, but going back to school again made me start thinking and I fear I probably confused myself in the process.

"Our people say that you greet the king of the spirits in a certain fashion. Ubelegede k'ana ekene eze muo. We were a people of order, and we had ways of doing things. The world made sense because we did not tell the truth and lie at the same time. If a man went to a shrine and swore an oath, you were reasonably certain that he was telling the truth. These days, the Today Today people, they swear the most spine-tingling oaths with the Bible – even when they're telling the emptiest lie. But even though we had our ways, we were not so set in them that we were incapable of change. We embraced change whenever it was good for us, not simply for the sake of form or to please new apostles. In fact, one of our most memorable proverbs is about change. Afu ife ka ubi elee oba. When a person sees something greater than his farm, he sells his barn. I think that was the proverb that Father liked most.

We were never perfect. We couldn't have been. And looking back now we seem even more imperfect. Hindsight is the king of naysayers.

"In those days, children were not given names before they were born. After they were born, they were named according to the life force within them. That was how Father was named Ileka because of the forcefulness of his aura. It was clear that he was born to strive and transcend. His father was a dibia, the priest of Ani, the grandson of Ikediani, the founder of our village. Ikediani, who was named after the power of the earth, led a migration in search of fertile farmlands. Ikediani and his group found what they were looking for in this area. But they also knew that there were forces in the world bigger or more powerful than them and that they needed to cultivate those forces. Ikediani went into the forest and returned with the symbol of the earth goddess. That was how he became her priest. So, right from the beginning, there was no king but there was a priest. And there was the earth goddess. If the village wanted to deliberate on an issue, it convoked an izu and every grown man had a say in that forum. If the men couldn't agree on what to do and the issue was serious enough, they sought the intervention of the earth goddess.

"Being the priest of Ani came with many responsibilities. The goddess ensured order; she rewarded good citizens and punished evildoers. Ikediani interpreted her wishes and made pronouncements on her behalf. She was beloved, but she was also feared. Ani blessed the earth and ensured a bountiful harvest. But if you went to the shrine of Ani and swore a false oath, she would strike you down. She meted justice as well as succor. It was also Ikediani's duty to ensure succession. His first child would inherit the office from him, and so on. So, when Father was born, he was destined to be the next priest of Ani. And after him his first child, your father. And after your father yourself, Ile. But that never happened. The chain of succession was broken, and the goddess lost her voice.

"Father had a very adventurous spirit, and as soon as he could he would walk long distances in search of who knows what. It was as if the village was too small for him and he was seeking a kind of expansion.

"'What is the matter with you?' his father would ask. 'You should be staying with me in the shrine more often and learning from me.'

"'I'm also learning outside the shrine.'

"'You're learning what?'

"'That the more we travel the bigger the world becomes.'

"'What does that mean? The shrine is your destiny, not wandering.'

"But I think Father was born a wanderer, and the beatings he received from his father could not still his wandering spirit. So, he was initiated into the ogba ngbada earlier than usual to immerse him in the ways of our people. Ikediani had emerged from the forest with two things – a symbol and a mask. The symbol became the icon of the goddess and remained in her shrine until it was destroyed by the madness of Isaiah. The mask was the medium through which spirits became men and men became spirits during the ogba ngbada dance. The ogba ngbada only appeared twice in those days – at the beginning and at the end of the hunting season. Farmers went to the earth goddess for blessings; hunters brought out the ogba ngbada to rally their spirits. But not all hunters were initiated into the ogba ngbada. It was a select brotherhood for those deemed worthy. If a man did very well, people said to him 'You're indeed an ogba ngbada' or 'You deserve to be an ogba ngbada,' because to be an ogba ngbada was to be a spirit without ceasing to be a man.

"Father did well as an ogba ngbada. He went to his first hunt when he was only ten years old, and he killed an antelope. It wasn't a lucky kill. He had to track this antelope, leaving his group behind. He could probably have shot other antelopes, but, no, he stayed with this particular one. People wondered why he did that.

"'Why did you go so far and risk so much to kill this antelope when you could perhaps have killed others with less effort?' they asked him.

"'But then I wouldn't have gone so far and risked so much.'

"'What does that mean?'

"'The joy is in the hunt, not the kill.'"

People looked at him and wondered if he was indeed only ten years old, but they knew the day he was born.

"'Your son is a bit strange,' they said to his father.

"'It's his ile,' he answered, not sure whether to be worried or proud. 'That's why I named him Ileka.'

"Father enjoyed the hunt and was gradually becoming a good acolyte in the shrine. He could already make divinations. And he could make rain. The priest of Ani was only required to act as the voice of the goddess, not also become a rainmaker. There were rainmakers, who claimed a different kind of gift. Some of them apparently made the rain fall or stop, but most of them were charlatans who engaged in all sorts of head-scratching performance. They would stare into the sky as if attempting to stare down an enemy, make wild gestures with their hands and feet, sometimes with their waists too, and shout or shoot into the air. If the rain still didn't fall or stop, they tried to explain their failure by referring to unseen forces.

"No one knows how Father learned to make rain, but he didn't put on a weird performance in order to do so. He would cusp his hands and whisper his secrets into them, then he would open his hands and blow them into the air. The rain clouds would begin to gather or the rain would taper off. He never accepted payments. He would listen to people's solicitations and then decide.

"'You want me to make rain to disrupt your enemy's funeral? I don't do that.'

"'Yes, I'll hold the rain for the ogba ngbada procession. Of course.'

"'Your sister's naming ceremony is right in the middle of the rainy season, but I promise you it won't rain in the afternoon. Only in the afternoon, because crops also need rain to grow.'

"'I can't make rain for your children to play in. They should go down to the river.'

"So, people consulted Father for all sorts of reasons, sometimes almost as much as they consulted his father. He rendered the services that agreed with his spirit, but he did not want any fee.

"'It's alright for a priest to receive tokens of appreciation, Ile,' his father advised him.

"'I'm not a priest.'

"'But you'll soon be.'

"He never did become a priest. For all his love of the rhythms and rituals of the village, the Catholic missionaries eventually snapped him up. I don't know if he believed in the stories they told about heaven and hell or if he was more fascinated by the distant journeys they promised. His father did everything he could to call him back to the shrine. He made it clear that his becoming a Christian did not mean that he disdained the shrine, but he could not be in two places at the same time. His father then presented other candidates to the earth goddess as his possible successors. But she rejected all of them. She wanted Father, no one else. By the time his father died, when Father was twelve years old, he was already in school and the shrine had no priest. His mother had died six years earlier. The first man who attempted to become the priest of Ani was struck dumb. Our people reasoned that the goddess might accept a woman instead, but the woman who tried to become her priestess went blind. Since then, the Ani shrine has been without a priest. People in the village still believe that the earth goddess cursed Father and the first-born offspring in his lineage. They believe that's why Father died and his corpse was never found and that's why your father went to bed and did not wake up at his age. And when you nearly cut off your friend's foot or almost killed a woman on campus, they said your own curse was a spurting madness."

"Is that true?" I couldn't help interrupting.

"Of course not," answered Aunt Rosette. "We've been washed clean by the blood of the Lamb. Fear not."

"I'm not really afraid."

"Good."

Ella pressed my hand in solidarity.

"I don't know what to think," Uncle Ibe said. "Our people say that no matter how fast a person is he cannot outrun his shadow. Sometimes, I wonder what happened to all the deities that we neglected. Since deities don't die, that means they must still be alive but we're no longer able to reach them and appeal to them if need be. So, maybe they knock us on the head sometimes. But if the Christians are to be believed, we now have a new aura, so perhaps the gods can't knock us on the head. Besides, is a god without worshippers still a god?"

"Did I hear you right, Ibe?"

"I said at the beginning that I've been pondering these things. And I'm still pondering. I still believe, but one person cannot make a village."

"Ikediani did."

"No, he was the leader of a group. Anyway, let's get back to Father. He did well as a Christian convert. The missionaries loved his zeal and his native knowledge. They saw in him a young man who could become a great evangelist, but he did not want to become a Catholic priest. If he had turned his back on his village priesthood, he did not want to become any other kind of priest. He did well in his studies, so well in fact that he eventually shipped out to study medicine in England. I think he wanted to visit every place on earth but he also realized that he couldn't, so he closed his eyes, spun around, and put a finger on a map. That way, everywhere on earth stood an equal chance. I think it also had to do with his evolving philosophy about the nature of our lives on earth."

"What if he had put a finger on a place that he couldn't go?"

"You still don't have a sense of the man? Father did not believe there was anything that he couldn't do. The idea itself probably never occurred to him. Once he made up his mind to do something, it was already done. He had the fire within him."

"Fire?"

"Yes – power, aura, spirit, force, whatever the right word is."

"He returned to Nigeria in the year of the country's Independence. He was the first black doctor in Fegge, the first to set up a hospital. It wasn't too big a hospital, but it always teemed with people."

"How was he able to set up a hospital immediately after medical school?"

"He didn't say, but it seems he returned from England with some money."

"But he went there to study, not to make money."

"Maybe he made money all the same. Or maybe he received help. Anyway, he realized right away that he couldn't run the hospital strictly on the principle of asking for due payment from every patient. He also didn't want to turn anyone away. So, he decided to charge his richer patients more and the poorer ones less.

"It was in the hospital that he met and married one of his patients. Mother said many people thought Father was a bit crazy. He sometimes stared at his patients too long, paced about unpredictably, hit his head while he was making a point, wrung his hands for no clear reason, and displayed other eccentricities. But he was a good doctor. Mother went there because she was having stomach pains. Father looked at her as if there was more than one of her in front of him, then jumped up and hit his forehead as if it was in the way, leaned forward and whispered to her.

"'You're the one.'

"She was bewildered. 'One...what?' she asked.

"'The one. I want to marry you.'

"Just like that?"

"Just like that."

"Mother was so alarmed that her stomach growled like a cornered animal. She ran out of the hospital and swore she would never go back. But Father ran after her. She was nimble and could run fast. Father was big, but he could also run fast. It was quite a spectacle. He caught up with her and carried her back, kicking, to the hospital. They were married within one month. Mother said, yes, Father was a bit crazy, but he made her feel blessed.

"Everything was going well until the Civil War broke out. Mother had a bad feeling about the war and didn't want Father to go.

"'What are you talking about, woman?' he demanded, looking at her as if she had lost her mind. 'Me, Ileka? I'm not a coward.'

"'Nobody is saying that you're a coward.'

"'Then what are you saying?'

"'It's the so-called cowards that stay home and survive with their families.'

"'And the so-called brave hearts die away from their families?'

"'I didn't say so.'

"'My dear, I'm not a coward. Besides, if I don't fight for Biafra, then why am I a man?'

"He left to volunteer, and they never saw each other again. Father came home at the end of the war. Mother died the previous month, in one of the last raids on Biafra. She had survived almost the entire war, shepherding us from place to place. The war was nearly over. She went to a makeshift market and a plane seemed to come out of nowhere and began strafing. Everyone ran. Mother fell.

"Father was inconsolable, and that word doesn't really express how brokenhearted he was. It was the only time that I ever saw him cry. 'Agha elie m!' he kept lamenting."

"That the war swallowed him?"

"Yes, that the war swallowed him. His coming back alive was meaningless to him if it was for the purpose of burying his wife. I don't think that Father was quite the same after that. I believe that something no one understood happened to him when Mother died. I mean, I've seen men bury their wives since then, but I've never seen any of them cry in that fashion. It was as if his very core had been wrenched out, and he lost some of his forcefulness. He would sometimes mope into the distance, muttering 'Agha elie m.' He talked about Lazarus at every opportunity."

"The Lazarus that was raised from the dead?"

"The same. He would recite the lines from the Bible: '*And when he thus had spoken, he cried with a loud voice, Lazarus, come forth. And he that was dead came forth, bound hand and foot with graveclothes: and his face was bound about with a napkin. Jesus saith unto them, Loose him, and let him go.*'

"That was how The Lazarus Project began. He stopped practicing as a doctor, entrusting that duty to other doctors that he employed. Instead, he invited people to bring their problems to him in his office. The war had ended not too long ago, and it was a time of great want and hopelessness. Every day, there was a long line of people waiting to see Father. If people had 'spiritual' problems, they went to the churches but if they had 'practical' problems, they came to see Father. These problems were often financial, and he appeared to be the only person in Fegge who had money and other forms of aid to share. He listened to everyone and helped those he could – often giving out money for purposes ranging from the next meal to managing terminal illnesses. He called it The Lazarus Project, and the idea was to help people begin new lives. But people began to call it King Lazarus, more in reference to the figure behind the benevolence project."

"How come he had so much money to share?"

"Maybe he received help. He made a trip to London after the war and when he came back he began The Lazarus Project."

"I thought he went to London only once – to go to school."

"No, he made a trip after the war – after months of mourning Mother intensely. He came back and he became King Lazarus. It didn't take long before people began to bring other kinds of problems to him. They wanted someone to talk to because they were going crazy thinking about their misfortunes. Father listened. They wanted someone to confide in because they had done something so terrible they couldn't tell even their priest. Father listened. They wanted advice on how to further their interests. Father listened and responded in whatever way he could to smoothen their paths."

"And he did all these in the hospital?"

"In the very same office where he had once applied the stethoscope, from the same chair that he had looked at Mother as if she were an irresistible incarnation."

"So, he was still a doctor?"

"No, the hospital was now being run by doctors on his staff. Well, you could say he was a doctor of souls. That was how his legend began. People came from everywhere to see him, and he tried not to let anyone go back without aid."

"He was a fixer?"

"I'm not sure that describes him well. Father never agreed to anything against his spirit and he never charged a fee. Some of those who came to see him wanted favors that he couldn't provide.

Those were the ones that he turned away."

"What kind of favors?"

"He said someone he knew wanted something he could slip into his wife's food or drink so that she would die without any suspicion falling on him.

"'Why would you want to do that?' he asked.

"'Because of her bad luck. She's sucking up my good luck, and that's why I'm not prospering.'

"'How do you know that? Did someone tell you that?'

"'The dibia, but he said my wife is so powerful in the coven of witches that he cannot kill her.'

"'You went to a dibia to kill your wife?'

"'I didn't know what else to do, then I thought of you.'

"'You're a fool, an animal. Listen to me carefully: I don't publicly discuss anyone who comes to me for help, but I'll visit your house every week. If your wife ever dies in a certain manner, I'll strangle you with my bare hands.'"

"Did he mean that?"

"Possibly. He had a list of people that he visited every week. It wasn't a long list, but he went to these houses until his death. It didn't take long for word to spread that if you wanted to harm anyone the worst person to tell was Father. So, that sort of traffic ceased."

"You skipped the moon landing," Aunt Rosette said to Uncle Ibe. "Quite surprising since you're the one who talks about it the most."

"True, my sister. I got carried away a bit. But our people say that if the eagle flies too fast it crashes into the sun."

"Ibe!"

"OK, I admit I made that up in a hurry," he said with a boyish smile, then he became serious. "We have to go back a little bit. Something else happened after Father came back from the war, something that I think was more important than we realized at the time. He picked up an old newspaper one day and his eyes almost popped out of his sockets. Please, don't think that's an exaggeration. I saw it happen. His eyeballs grew so big I thought they would explode. He was reading the news about the first man on the moon. He read the paragraphs in the paper as if the words were inexhaustible. He read and read and read, then he exhaled a windy rush of air.

"'A man walked on the moon,' he said with limitless amazement. 'A *man* walked on the moon. A man *walked* on the moon. A man walked *on* the moon. A man walked on *the moon*. A man walked on the moon? A man walked on the moon. A man walked on the moon!'"

"We all feared he was going mad. He was so dazed by the news that we were unsure what he would do next. Father wasn't the sort of person who did nothing."

"What did he do?"

"That's the thing. He didn't do anything. He did buy a new atlas though, a bigger atlas than the one he used to decide to go to London. But all he did was study that atlas, study it so much that we joked that Father must know the world better than anyone who had traveled it."

"Was that why he left?" Ella asked slowly. "A man walked on the moon in 1969, and he left in 1974."

"That's where the story gets murky. But why would he leave because of that?"

"Because he felt challenged."

"To do what – walk on the moon?"

"In his own way."

"Even the people that go to walk on the moon return to their families, but Father's been gone for forty-four years."

"I can't believe that he would leave us just like that."

"Me too."

"Why not? He killed an antelope and could make rain at

ten; he was an orphan at twelve. And he coped, even though his father didn't own a hospital or King Lazarus. He probably believed that you could cope."

"Really? He was a family man, someone who cared deeply about his family. That's why Mother's death affected him so much. I don't believe he would abandon us like that."

"Or maybe you don't want to believe it."

"Ile!"

I apologized.

"Your father was only thirteen years old at the time. In what part of the world is a thirteen-year-old boy considered so grown that his father would leave him to fend for himself and two siblings?"

"Maybe he meant to return."

"No, Father died in 1974, and we buried him in 1981."

"1981? Seven years later? I thought he was buried the same year he died. Why would there be a seven-year gap between his death and his funeral?"

"Like I said, this is where the story gets murky, so pay attention. As Father studied his atlas, he became calmer, almost as if he was waiting for something. We were happy that he had found something that had a calming effect on him. Then the year before he died, something happened that rooted his legend. An epidemic broke out in Isiani and the neighboring villages. No one could explain it. People were dropping dead as if it was a new kind of performance, except that none of the dead ever came back. Something seemed to be swirling in the air, and whoever caught it began to cough, then develop reddish eyes, dry up, and die. The Christians chanted that it was the judgment of God. Some villagers said it was the vengeance of the earth goddess. Whatever it was was a tone-deaf killer; it was unmoved by supplications and lamentations. People began to flee the villages. The public health workers who were supposed to investigate the cause of the epidemic and how to resolve it refused to set foot in any of the villages. They quarantined refugees from these villages who fled to the city and interviewed them. Based on this 'field research,' they wrote reports and recommendations that no one apparently read. No help came.

"When Father heard of the nature and extent of the epidemic, he said thoughtfully: 'A man will set forth.'"

"What man?"

"Himself. 'A man will set forth.' He turned toward the very place that people were scrambling to flee and he set forth. He went to Isiani and examined the afflicted as if he was impervious to the rampage of the epidemic. That same night, he went into the thickest forest. No one knew what he was looking for. He came out of the forest three nights later..."

"'He came out of the forest.' 'He came out of the night.' That's it?"

"Yes, some people prefer to say that he came out of the forest, others that he came out of the night. Virtually no one says he came out of the forest at night, but that's what happened. He had found the source of the epidemic at the point where our people say that the forest 'dips into' the river. That was how the epidemic was stopped. He saved entire villages when no one else cared whether our people lived or died. Some of the villagers think he's a spirit in the shape of a man.

"When he returned home, he took up his atlas again and he wrote: 'A man set forth.'"

"Really?"

"'A man set forth.' I saw it myself. You see, your father was quite well-behaved and usually did as Father told him. Your auntie here sometimes behaved and sometimes didn't—"

"Ibe!"

"I don't mean any disrespect. Our people say..."

"Again?"

Ibe reconsidered. "I was the one whom Father believed had plastic ears. Whatever he told me not to do, that was exactly what I had to do. I don't understand it now, but that was the way it was. So, 'Be sure you don't touch that atlas, otherwise I'll teach you a lesson' sounded like 'Please do as you wish with that atlas, otherwise I'll teach you a lesson.' I saw the words myself: 'A man will set forth,' then 'A man set forth.' I thought, well, that's what travel is all about: someone sets forth. Later, those words would haunt me – not the one in Father's atlas but the ones uttered by Ije on his deathbed."

"Who's Ije?"

"He was our kinsman. Ije and Father have a history. Ije went to King Lazarus one day and asked Father to lend him money. He said he was planning a thanksgiving ceremony to celebrate his promotion to an elder in the Jesus Jesus Church. Father listened patiently, then he explained to Ije that he was not a moneylender; he only helped people with their needs, not their wants. Ije insisted that the thanksgiving ceremony was a need. Father didn't think so. When he couldn't convince Father, Ije became insolent. He said he didn't know what devil pushed him into coming to Father in the first place. How could a heathen like him, a village priest without a shrine, comprehend that a church thanksgiving was a spiritual need? Father listened to him for a few minutes, then he stood up and dragged Ije out of his office into the street. Ije told everyone who cared to listen that he had disowned Father as a kinsman. Father did not care to respond.

"The next year, the same Ije was back at King Lazarus. He needed a loan – he stressed the word 'need' – to pay his hospital bill. Father listened to him patiently, as if Ije had not said the most terrible things about him. Then he told Ije that he was not a moneylender but that he would pay the hospital bill. Ije said he did not accept handouts; he needed a loan. Maybe because of Ije's condition, Father made an exception and gave him a loan. Ije defaulted. He asked for a deferment, and Father told him to pay back when he could."

"Did he ever pay back?"

"He kept saying that he would, but he never did."

"How did he become involved in the search?"

"He volunteered. He was one of the leaders of the search because he worked at the bus station. The reasoning was that if Father had traveled or was taken out of Fegge, maybe someone at the bus station saw him. But Ije was the person who instead asked that we stop the search for Father because he must already be dead. Otherwise, how could a masquerade like Father be missing? Maybe he was a spirit all along and had returned to the spirit world. People were surprised, because Ije was an elder in the Jesus Jesus Church and not someone who ever talked of masquerades and spirits.

"A few years later, when Ije realized he was going to die from the illness that had kept him in bed for weeks, he muttered weakly 'There's something I have to say...' He seemed to realize that he didn't have enough time, so he added as quickly as he could, 'A man set forth.' People didn't understand the connection, so they thought he was delirious or that maybe he was announcing his own setting forth. Maybe. I couldn't stop thinking about those words. I'm not sure anyone else knew that Father used those words. So, how had Ije known? What had he wanted to say that he had kept bottled up previously? But why ask all these questions? I told myself. Sometimes, we have to accept things the way they are, even though it can be difficult to do so. The thing about certain kinds of questions is that they don't yield answers. They just whir in your head, but they're not airplanes so you're still where you are. No matter how much a penguin flaps its wings, it cannot fly."

"Penguin? You have a proverb with a penguin in it?"

He laughed. "So, you think you're the only one with a ticket to travel the world these days?"

"Anyway, you skipped the most important part of the story.

How did Grandfather die?"

"He disappeared..."

"You see, he liked to take walks in the evenings," Aunt Rosette took over. "Every evening, he would take a walk around the neighborhood, then return home in time for dinner. After dinner, he would watch the television or read the newspaper or tell us stories. On this evening, he went out as usual, and that was the last time we saw him. At first, we thought he had been delayed, but he didn't come back that night or the next day or ever."

"Could he have been kidnapped?"

"Only in theory. It's difficult to imagine Father coming to any harm in Fegge. Besides, he was not a man to trifle with."

"What about the missing body?"

"That's a deep puzzle, and that's why we searched for him with determination. The whole of Fegge and Isiani, as well as its surrounding villages, took part in the search year after year. But sometimes there are things that we cannot know. It's the world."

"Did he go out with anything that evening?"

"Nothing, except his atlas. But that wasn't unusual. He carried it everywhere."

"So, how did he go from 'missing' to 'dead'?"

"It's been forty-four years. In Isiani, we search for a missing person for four or seven years, depending. After that, we hold a funeral. In Father's case, God knows we looked everywhere. Someone even went to London to make inquiries. No one had seen him. No one had heard of him. We buried him seven years after he disappeared."

"But he could still have been alive then?"

"In theory."

People talked about my grandfather all the time, I thought, but there was so much that they did not talk about.

"How come no one told me all this until today?"

"Because we didn't want to encumber you with questions

without answers. You're the new generation. Besides, we had already buried Father according to our custom. If he came back after that we would have to 'unbury' him for him to be 'alive' again."

"But, in your hearts, did you really think that he was dead?"

"Of course," Aunt Rosette answered immediately. "Of course."

"Yes, without a question," said Uncle Ibe. But it seemed to me there was a question even in his answer.

"There's one more thing," he said. "I don't know if this is relevant or not, but since it's somehow connected to Father's atlas in my mind I might as well mention it. I looked at that atlas a few times..."

"A *few* times?" asked Aunt Rosette.

"Quite a few times then, but it's not as if I ever borrowed or stole it. One of the times I went to look at it, there was an envelope on top of it, and it was addressed to Father. On the left-hand side was a name, Ann Pottinger, with a foreign address. I think there was 'London' in that address. On the right-hand side was a stamp with a picture of the Queen of England."

"Are you sure of these details, uncle?"

"It was a very long time ago, but I'm quite sure of the name – Ann Pottinger. It has a certain ring."

"Did you mention these to Auntie then?"

"The name, yes – Ann Pottinger," said my aunt. "The other details, he mentioned them too but not with the same certainty."

"What's the connection between the envelope and the atlas?"

"Maybe nothing, but that was the only time I saw anything on top of that atlas. Maybe it was important, maybe it wasn't."

"Father never mentioned that name," Aunt Rosette added, "and we concluded it probably wasn't important."

"Where's the envelope and the letter inside it?"

"The envelope disappeared. I never saw it again. The letter was never there. I mean there should have been a letter inside the envelope, but it wasn't there even then."

Ann Pottinger. What, if anything, could this mean, I wondered? Was my uncle somehow mistaken? I doubted that, especially if he had told the same story to Aunt Rosette forty-four years ago. Why did they remember the name so clearly? Was it simply because they still remembered? I had never heard my grandfather associated with any other woman than my grandmother, so was this something worthy of further attention? Did "Ann Pottinger" even refer to a real person or could it be a pseudonym? I decided I would try to find out. I would try to find out as much as I could about the unknown life or lives of my grandfather.

Afu ife ka ubi elee oba.

After our meeting, Uncle Ibe said he would remain behind in the village for some time to rest and drink "original" palm wine.

"You're always staying behind in the village to rest," Aunt Rosette told him. "Are you fighting the battle of your life somewhere?"

"Thou hast said it thyself," he replied. "The world is too bogus not to long for the village. Unfortunately, the village itself is becoming kind of bogus."

"Are you sure you won't change your mind?"

"Why all the fuss? Have you forgotten the way to Abuja? If you have, then you're lost because I never knew the way myself."

We all laughed.

"You want to abandon your family in Abuja?" Aunt Rosette asked.

"Tufia! That's why I keep going back."

Aunt Rosette left for Abuja with Ella, who wanted to see Nigeria's capital city, and I traveled to Fegge to see Lawyer Egwuatu. His name was Fabian Egwuatu, but people called him Lawyer Egwuatu because he usually did not let anyone forget that he was an attorney. He was known to respond to concerns or threats with a response that was also his name – "Egwu atu?" – which could mean anything from "Is he not afraid of me?" to "Are they not afraid of us?" He was a short man who, in his heyday, was known in Fegge for his style – his Afro, the way he parted his hair, the white shirt and long tie that he favored, and his pants that barely reached his ankles, revealing his cotton socks and shining shoes in their full splendor. He walked in a way that made people unsure if he was affecting a future limp or a present swagger. When he spoke, people said his diction made an advanced dictionary necessary to understand some of his words. He was my grandfather's attorney, which was not surprising because Egwuatu later became a legal luminary in the region, one of the few attorneys to argue – and win – cases before the Supreme Court. What was surprising was that my grandfather chose him when he could have had any attorney in the region, when Egwuatu was just out of law school and still chasing ambulances for potential clients.

"In fact," said Egwautu himself, because he loved to tell the story, "I almost had a cardiovascular eruption when he entrusted me with the office."

He had gone to see King Lazarus after law school because he did not have money to pay the rent for the one room he occupied in a high-density house known as "Face me I face you." He didn't like having to queue up in the morning to use the bathroom or having to rush out because the next person on the queue was already screaming "Abeg, come out, Lawyer, this na public toilet no be court o," but it was the only accommodation he could barely afford at the time. He waited impatiently as the queue outside King Lazarus moved slowly because my grandfather insisted on personally attending to everyone who came to see him.

By afternoon, Egwuatu was so hungry that he was yawning shamelessly. He was bothered less by the yawns than by the fact that he had no money either to go to a restaurant or to the market to buy foodstuff. He still had some garri and water in his room, and his only option was to soak that and drink, maybe with a few pieces of fried groundnut. He had been doing that for a whole week, and he was sick and tired of even the idea.

He had become so broke that his appearance, which he usually invested in, was showing the signs. Because he could no longer afford to buy soap, he had started bathing and washing his clothes with only water. His white shirt, which used to gleam from a distance, now looked like something that had been picked up from a gutter and washed in the morning dew. His Afro, unmistakably oiled in less gloomy times, now looked like an old wig purchased at a discounted price at Ochanja Market. As he stood or sat – because he did more sitting on the ground than standing, ignoring inquiring glances and questions – he was under no illusion that he had other options. King Lazarus was his "last bus stop." He couldn't go home to his destitute parents, who had been unable to help pay his tuition in school but had hoped that his graduation would mark a new dawn for the family. The last time he went home to see them and suggested that his father sell his only land – including the mud hut that he lived in with his mother – so that he could rent "decent accommodation" for the family, he had told him something that kept him awake at night.

"Listen here, you idiot. If you ever come back here to ask me for anything, anything at all, I'll curse you with my left hand on the ground. Everything we had we already gave you. Maybe it wasn't much, but that was everything we had to give."

Egwuatu was bothered that his father had threatened to curse him. Why not disown him? A curse had a ring of finality to it whereas being disowned sounded like something that could be discussed when tempers cooled down. A curse could require reversal rituals to annul. And a left hand on the ground? What did that even mean? Had his father become left-handed from a special species of poverty or was a curse with a left hand on the ground more devastating than one with a right hand?

Despite what people considered a cavalier attitude, Egwuatu was someone who sometimes thought deeply into the night. Lately, a thought had begun to occur to him that scared him. All his problems stemmed from his existence, he had decided. He was born into a family that was poorer than the common sense of "poor" and he had the luck of the devil: nothing that he attempted, and he had attempted numerous things, ever seemed to work out. So, the idea occurred to him that the solution might be to void his existence, to tie a rope around his neck and hang himself. No suicide note required. Surely, everyone in Fegge would know why. He might leave a note to spite the landlord, who seemed to especially enjoy harassing him to pay his rent at the end of the month, reminding him just last week that he owed more than six months already. As if he didn't know. As if he wanted to owe any rent at all or live in a "Face me I face you." But why bother? Besides, the landlord was only doing what he had to, and he had been considerate enough not to evict him yet.

He dispelled the thought as vigorously as he could and woke up early the next morning to line up in front of King Lazarus. It was Egwuatu's pride that had prevented him from doing so previously. He was sure that everyone in Fegge knew he was destitute, but so far it was a speculation, an allegation. To be seen in that queue would provide the missing evidence for his sentencing. His pride, though in tatters, had struggled against that.

When Egwuatu entered my grandfather's office, he quickly kneeled down and began to rattle off his woes. He had no intention of getting up on his feet again until my grandfather parted the waves or simply did something to make his life less miserable. But he was dealing with a man who was not always subtle. My grandfather physically lifted him up and sat him down on the chair.

"No need to kneel," he said. "Speak with your mouth, not

your knees."

Egwuatu feared he had made a catastrophic blunder. How could he repair the damage? But...what had he done wrong?

"Besides," my grandfather said to him, "what I see in you is greater than what you are."

Egwuatu pricked his ears as if he was hearing a new language that he had not known existed. He had become accustomed to bamboozling people in Fegge with his occasional bombast, but he had no idea what my grandfather was talking about. "What I see in you is greater than what you are." Had he missed his way and ended up at a diviner's?

"You don't understand..." he began again, foregoing any big words.

"I do, more than you know."

"Excuse me, sir, do you know me?"

"I've seen you before, I think, but that's not what I mean."

"Sir..."

Grandfather hit his forehead, leaned over and almost whispered. "It's you."

"Me?"

"Yes, I want you to be my lawyer."

Egwuatu quickly looked behind him to make sure there were only two of them in the room. Despite his verbal acrobatics, no one had ever asked him to be his attorney in that manner. How could King Lazarus choose him, and just like that?

From that day on, Egwuatu promised, his words gushing like a waterfall tumbling with joy at the sight of the river below, he would have only one client, one that he would willingly lay down his life for if need be. "No," my grandfather told him, "you should have other clients. You're a lawyer, and others need you too. And please don't lay down your life for me. All I want is your service and friendship." Egwuatu was stupefied. King Lazarus had asked for his service. "Of course!" And friendship. "Forever!"

Egwuatu's fortune improved so dramatically that his father was happy to welcome him back with an outpouring of blessings. But some of his old swagger was gone. He had swaggered out of law school and been so humbled by life that it kind of changed the way he looked at things. My grandfather hardly went to court, but Egwuatu was always busy attending to his "interests." It was not clear why my grandfather needed an attorney in the first place, not to talk of one that he sometimes spent hours in his office discussing God knows what. Whenever anyone dared ask Egwuatu what he was "lawyering" for King Lazarus, he would query back: "Have you never been acquainted with the customary confidentiality of attorney-client privilege?" "Carry go!" some people responded, a popular expression that could mean anything from "You're OK" to "Avaunt!"

When my grandfather disappeared, Egwuatu was like a general commanding the troops in the search for a field marshal. He put full-page advertisements in the newspapers and even traveled to London to make inquiries. I couldn't help wondering: Was it all an act? If he had been as close to my grandfather as everyone said, why did my grandfather not reveal his intentions to him?

Egwuatu looked at me for a long time after I asked him that question.

"I look at you and I see your grandfather," he said to me. "So, I won't take offense. I'm a man of integrity. That was what your grandfather saw in me the very first day that we met. If I knew his plan – that is, if what you say has any locus standi, which I aver to the contrary that it doesn't – I wouldn't have told anyone, but I wouldn't put on a show, as you implied."

I apologized. "Where could he have gone?" I asked him.

"I believe he died. I don't know how. There's no other explanation."

I had already shown him the picture that Willem sent to

me from South Africa, but he had dismissed it as "an astonishing resemblance, a questionable correlation." Why were they – my uncle, my aunt, and my grandfather's attorney – determined not to consider the possibility that my grandfather went away and continued to exist somewhere else before and after they held a funeral for him? Why were they "in denial," as we would sometimes say at an anger management class about people who disputed their circumstances regardless of the evidence?

"Did anything happen just before his disappearance – the day or the week or the month before?"

He simply shook his head, which could have meant "Nothing" or "It's privileged information."

"Did he change his will, for instance?"

"He never had one."

"He must have had a will. I understand you were the executor."

"I mean, he didn't have a will until the week before he disappeared. He called me in, a few days before that day and dictated, then later signed his will."

I was so surprised that I didn't know how to respond.

"We've discussed the will before, but we didn't get around to formalizing it until then. It was a simple will. He left everything he had to his children but also gave me a generous allowance and made a provision for King Lazarus. I was to be his children's guardian if anything happened to him before they were of age."

"And something happened."

"Sadly. But the children turned out alright, even Ibe. I did my best. It was the only way I could pay back a man who practically saved my life and to whom I pledged undying friendship."

"You said *even* Ibe. What happened to him?"

"I think he took his father's disappearance too much to heart, maybe because he was the youngest. He used to show up almost every day in this house to ask me to 'do more to bring him home.' Then, one day, he stopped coming. He had vanished."

"To where?"

"He walked all the way back to the village, fourteen miles, managed to break into the house, and began to live there. He was only eleven years old at the time. He stopped going to school and became a palm wine tapper. Can you imagine that? Every time I went to the village to bring him back, he would disappear into the forest and stay there for days. He was determined not to come back to the city until I 'brought back' his father."

"How did he survive as a palm wine tapper?"

"We thought he wouldn't, but he's as tough as your grandfather. He also fell in love with the village, so much so that he had no intention of ever leaving."

"You went to London to look for my grandfather?"

"Yes, I did. It was the only other place he had been to outside Nigeria. I went to his old school to ask around, even check if he had re-enrolled."

"You thought that was a possibility?"

"Not really, but we did everything that we could to find him. I'm sure of that. I put advertisements in British newspapers, searched out Nigerians and other people who knew him. No one had seen him or heard of him recently."

"But they could have seen him and not told you?"

"Why would they do that? And I did a lot more than just go to London to ask questions. I was able to check airport departure records back in Nigeria. Your grandfather never left the country."

"How were you able to do that?"

"You can't even imagine the lengths we went to to find your grandfather."

"But he could have left without..."

"Let it go," he said. "We did everything that could be done.

Your grandfather died in 1974. We don't know how, but no other explanation is possible. Besides, how could such a man, a gargantuan entity, an exemplary colossus, have become invisible and inaudible if still alive?"

"Did you speak to Ann Pottinger?"

"Who's she?"

"I don't know. I'm trying to find out who she is or if she even exists."

"We searched everywhere, in all directions, both longitudinally and latitudinally," he assured me.

It occurred to me that in a neighborhood noted for markets as well as churches, Egwuatu might have profited even more from his love of bombast if he had applied it from the pulpit. I could almost hear him across the road from the Jesus Jesus Church responding to every incantatory oh-la-la from Pastor Isaiah with an untranslatable speechification.

When I made to leave, he insisted that I stay for lunch.

"You, the grandson of Ileka, cannot come to my house and leave without some substantial nourishment," he insisted.

"I already ate."

"But not in my domain."

"But..."

"God blessed and translated me through your grandfather. He infused me with a surplus dynamism. The least I can do is offer you a miserly meal."

The meal was definitely not miserly. There was so much food on the table that I didn't know whether to admire the array or to attempt to actually eat. If people ate like this all the time or even half the time, I mused, they couldn't be very productive.

"Eat, eat," he encouraged, "life is short."

And it could be shorter, I thought, if indeed I ate according to his encouragement.

"Have you heard the story of Ojadili?" he asked me as we

ate.

"No, why?"

"It was one of the many stories your grandfather told me. I'll tell you the story, and then I'll tell you why or what I think.

"Once upon a time, there was a wrestler known as Ojadili. He was so good in the arena that he had defeated all the challengers in his village, so he was the unrivaled champion. No one had ever seen such a wrestler. But Ojadili wanted to be a champion beyond his village. So, he set off to find other challengers in other villages. He was a man fully awakened by the thrill of the arena. He traveled far and defeated every challenger wherever he went. Ojadili was so good in the arena that he invented a new challenge. He began to fight multiple challengers – two challengers, three challengers, four challengers, five challengers, six challengers, seven challengers – and he defeated them all. He was now a champion in all the known world, east to west, north to south. He was so accomplished that if he had dared an entire village to a challenge, no one would have had the courage to step into the arena.

"But the arena still called. Ojadili then decided to do something that had never been done. He would travel to the land of the spirits and challenge them to a wrestling match. Surely, that would establish him as the greatest wrestler ever, both in the land of the living and the land of the spirits. When his mother found out his intention, she begged him not to go; she told him that to challenge the spirits to a wrestling match could only end tragically. But Ojadili insisted that he must go. He could already hear the roar of the crowd beside the wrestling arena. So, his mother begged him not to go until he had eaten his favorite meal. She then put a stone into a pot of water and began to boil it. The stone boiled and boiled. She hoped Ojadili would come to his senses while waiting. But the more he waited the more his spirit was fired up. He could even hear the people chanting his praise name as he returned from the land of the spirits a hero:

Ojadili!
Ngolodi Ngolodidi Ngolo-lo
Ojadili!

"When he could not wait anymore, Ojadili left without his mother's knowledge. He traveled across seven lands and seven rivers to get to the land of the spirits. Once there, he challenged the spirits to wrestling matches to determine who was superior. But they only laughed at his impudence. He challenged them again, boasting that he had never been defeated and could never be defeated. So, they brought out a spirit with one head to wrestle with him and teach him a lesson. But, to everyone's surprise, Ojadili won. They brought out a spirit with two heads. It looked even more terrible than the last spirit. Still, Ojadili won. They brought a spirit with three heads, four heads, five heads, six heads. Each spirit was more terrible and capable than the last one. But it didn't matter how frightening each spirit looked or how it was – whether it could emit fire or was scalier than a crocodile – Ojadili defeated them all. At last, the spirits decided to bring out his chi, a smallish spirit with seven heads that it could barely carry. Ojadili laughed and made to pick up this spirit and smash it. But the spirit lifted only one finger, and it smashed Ojadili on the ground with its smallest finger."

We ate in silence for some time while I pondered the story. My grandfather had almost become the priest of the earth goddess, so he knew a lot about our folklore and had learned all sorts of hidden knowledge. What was this story meant to say to me, and why had my grandfather told it to Egwuatu?

"Now, the why," Egwuatu said. "Your grandfather told me many stories. He was a spectacular man, but sometimes he simply liked to talk. I remember the Ojadili story because of some of your questions. I used to think that your grandfather was a bit like Ojadili because he had an iron will and a wandering spirit, but he wasn't vainglorious. I feared that one day this world, this small world that we know, would become too small for him."

"You think that's what happened?"

"No, that's what I used to think before I knew him well. Afterward, I thought that, unlike Ojadili, his own journey was in a reverse direction. He was a spirit who crossed into the world of the living and his mission was to uplift, to raise the dead. It appears you think otherwise, but Ojadili is not who your grandfather was deep within him."

I didn't know what to think.

I left Egwuatu feeling that I didn't learn everything that I could have from him, and it was not because he was unwilling to talk. Perhaps I hadn't asked all the right questions or made the right interpretations. Or maybe I liked him – he was a jolly good fellow – more than I agreed with some of his own interpretations.

HOUSTON, July 20 - Two men landed on the moon today and for more than two hours walked its forbidding surface in mankind's first exploration of an alien world.

In the most incredible adventure in human history, these men coolly established earth's first outpost in the universe, sending back an amazing panorama of views to millions of awed TV viewers.

With his camera recording the fantastic, totally unreal scene for his home planet, Apollo 11 commander Neil Armstrong climbed down a nine-rung ladder from the cabin of the landing craft called Eagle, and became the first man to step on the moon. It was 10:56 p.m., New York time.

"That's one small step for man, one giant leap for mankind," Armstrong exclaimed.

Nineteen minutes later, Edwin E. (Buzz) Aldrin Jr. joined

Armstrong on the surface, and cried: "Beautiful, beautiful, beautiful, a magnificent desolation."

In the two hours and 16 minutes between the time Armstrong stepped on the surface and the pair were back inside Eagle's cabin, research was begun. It may unlock many secrets of the universe and provide clues to how it all started.
– New York Daily News, *July 21, 1969*

"Your grandfather was Ojadili, but he wasn't?" Ella asked me on the phone. "What are you talking about?"

"Perhaps my grandfather was sui generis. He wasn't a priest, but he was a priest; he was Lazarus, but he wasn't Lazarus; he was Ojadili, but he wasn't Ojadili; he was a spirit, but he wasn't a spirit. The more I learn about him, the more questions I have."

"Remember what Uncle Ibe said. To some questions, there are no answers. It's the world."

"You almost sound like him."

We laughed.

"I can't believe it's been six days already. Soon, it'll be time to go back to Houston."

"Have you called Sal to remind her to pick you up?"

"I called her, and *she* reminded me about my return date."

"Vintage Sal."

"Have you spoken with Joel and Nathan?"

"I'll call them today."

Ella was due back the next day, after spending three days in Abuja, and we would then travel together to Lagos. From there, she would travel back to Houston and I would leave for Stellenbosch. Uncle Ibe had decided to stay back in the village until we left for Lagos. "Just to make sure you're alright," he said. I didn't doubt him, but he also seemed to be having a good time in the village – drinking palm wine as if it was about to be prohibited and eating "bush meat" – grass cutter, antelope, bush pig – as if he was at a lavish ogba ngbada festival at the beginning of time. "It's the way the world was given to us," he would sometimes say. His world was obviously not my grandfather's, I thought. He did not own an atlas and was unlikely to ever do so. I once asked him if there was any circumstance under which he would get on a plane. "Of course," he said, his eyes glistening with mischief. "If the plane is on the ground and guaranteed to remain there." After we stopped laughing, he said: "My dear, a bird flies; a man watches and shakes his head. If you swim the river as if it is a pond, it will swallow you like an ocean." I was no longer sure what he was talking about. My uncle could be confusing sometimes. When I reminded him that Aunt Rosette's husband was a pilot, so we had a flier in the family, he said "God bless him. It's the way the world was given unto him."

I called Nathan after I spoke with Ella to let him know what progress I had made in my quest. He was amazed that I had been able to learn so much in such a short time.

"Are you satisfied now?" he asked me.

I was puzzled by the question. "What do you mean?"

"Is it all worth it?"

"You don't sound excited."

"I'm happy your journey so far hasn't been in vain, but sometimes after you acquire something you kind of ask yourself: 'What now?'"

"Next stop: South Africa."

"I know, but that's not what I mean. Anyway, we'll talk when you get back to Lagos."

"Certainly."

I called Joel, and he listened to me patiently as I complained that no one – not even Nathan – seemed excited about what I now considered the great quest of my life.

"Well, Nathan never knew your grandfather. I'm sure he's

happy for you, but it's difficult to get excited about something that happened forty-four years ago unless it has something to do with you personally."

"But this has something to do with me personally."

"Maybe."

"What do you mean?"

"I mean, you've lived thirty-three years believing that your grandfather was dead. The question really is: Why are you excited to learn that his death date has changed?"

"Because I want to know – no, to understand – what happened in between."

"Why?"

"I want to understand him."

"Is that possible?"

"I'll try my best."

I considered what Joel had said. "But what about the people who actually knew him?" I asked. "They're determined not to consider the possibility that he didn't die when they thought he did."

"People are different. Some other people might be fascinated. But consider too that grief is such a powerful thing. The passing of a loved one provokes perhaps the deepest kind of grief. After your uncle and auntie have grieved and recomposed themselves for so long, someone calls and says 'Oh, your father didn't die then, he just died yesterday.' Too many questions float up, and I'm sure they're dealing with those in their own way. But why start all over again? Their reaction would probably have been different if the call had been to say that your grandfather is still alive in South Africa. You know, I've seen many kinds of people in my consulting room. Some are driven crazy because they want to know everything that can be known. Some others accept that everything can't be known."

"But it's important to know as much as possible."

"Ultimately. I'm on your side, Ile."

I felt a bit better after speaking with Joel.

I felt much better after visiting King Lazarus with Ella. The hospital had been renovated a number of times since the days of my grandfather. My father had preferred to do so than to rebuild so as to maintain some of the architectural features – the wide verandas, the gabled roof, the curvy exterior – of an age gone by. He had considered the building "a Fegge heritage." My aunt did not disagree, but she had wanted to rebuild the hospital. I kept telling her I would think about it. Then, I was neither committed to maintaining the heritage nor changing it, but I kept deferring making a final decision. I was happy I did so. My grandfather's hospital was one of the few houses in Fegge that not only evoked an age gone by but was reminiscent of a time when building a house was a painstaking process instead of quickly piling blocks together, applying cement like toothpaste, and then hoping that no one died if or when the so-called construction came tumbling down. The building had become such a Fegge landmark that I could not imagine the neighborhood without it after I properly understood why it meant so much to many people. King Lazarus was not simply a hospital; it was also – or maybe even more – about the man behind it all.

If the building still remained the same, however, almost everything else had changed. My father had remodeled my grandfather's office. Aunt Rosette, who used that same office when she visited, had changed it according to her taste after my father died. Even the desk and chair that my grandfather had used had been removed. I had hoped to show Ella something in the office that dated back to the time of my grandfather, but virtually everything seemed to have changed.

My grandfather had employed other doctors to run the hospital while he personally saw to the King Lazarus charity. My father loved being a doctor; he also loved the charity. So, he did both, employing doctors and other workers in the hospital and the charity to assist him. He also stopped requiring people to come and see him personally. My aunt was neither a doctor nor someone who particularly believed in charity. My grandfather's will ruled out closing King Lazarus. Besides, I was neither in agreement nor disagreement then with that possibility, so my aunt gradually transformed the charity into a different kind of institution. She still aided the neediest but chose to "invest" instead in others. Under her care, King Lazarus became a moneylender of sorts, the very thing my grandfather had said that he wasn't.

Through all these changes, one thing remained constant: King Lazarus was about raising the dead, in a sense: "I am the resurrection and the life." It mostly helped those who had exhausted almost all other options or had none. It struck me then, as it never did in all those years, that this was my grandfather's priesthood. He did become a village priest after all, but his shrine was different from his father's. And he did become a Catholic priest too, but his altar was different from the missionaries'. It was now up to me to keep that mission alive and I would do so with a new spirit, I decided during that visit with Ella.

"What do you plan to do?" my aunt asked. "People simply keep coming back. Some of them have had three organ transplants or buried six mothers or have four fathers in emergency wards or whatever story they need to get money out of King Lazarus. It goes on and on. If we invest rather than gift, we help them strive and thrive; in return, we get our investment back, no interest. That's actually a great favor. Father used to say that the world is always changing. I don't believe he would be doing the same thing after forty years if he were still alive. The war ended a long time ago, so people are not as destitute today as they were after the war ended."

I wasn't sure my grandfather would have approved. "We'll talk more about this, auntie, after my trip to South Africa," I told her.

She wished me well in South Africa.

Uncle Ibe did the same. On the day Ella and I left for Lagos, he said to me: "I hope you found some of the answers that you came for, Ile. Your grandfather was too spectacular for any simple story. He was a man among men, but maybe sometimes he forgot that he was still a man, one man."

Ella said she thoroughly enjoyed visiting Nigeria – "Lagos, Isiani, Abuja, everywhere" – but she was looking forward to returning to Houston.

"Really, without me?"

"Look at you! Of course not. You know what I mean."

"I thought you were ready to return to Nigeria with me to live?"

"Anytime. Just not this week."

We both laughed.

My visit to Nigeria had been quite revealing. I hoped I would find more answers in South Africa.

The Book of Everything

I arrived in Cape Town en route to Stellenbosch expectantly. I wanted to learn a lot more about my grandfather. But that was the great expectation. The immediate one was being able to recognize Willem, whom I had never seen. He had told me he would pick me up at the airport and that he would be carrying a nameplate. I had responded that there was no need for that, that I would be able to recognize him.

"You think so?" he asked me.

I assured him that I would. I had spoken with him a number of times, and I prided myself on being able to visualize people without having met them. Sometimes, I would hear a song on the radio and I would describe to Ella or Joel what the musician, whom I had never seen, looked like. At times, we even made a bet before looking up the artist. I won more bets than I lost. Occasionally, my description would be so off that Joel would say that taking my money was almost like stealing. I would then study the picture of the artist as if it had a confession to make to me.

"Are you sure this fellow actually sang that song or maybe she was lip-synching?"

"Don't be a sore loser," Joel would say.

Sometimes, I wondered: "How are we sure this guy has not had cosmetic surgery? He doesn't at all look like the guy who sang that song."

"Ile," Ella would say coolly, "that's the singer alright. And you owe me."

"You're a gambler, you know," I would tease her.

"Two of us, and right now I'm on the winning side of the table."

I had bet against myself this time. When I walked into the arrival hall and saw people holding up nameplates, I decided I would not look at the names. I would look at the people themselves, pick out Willem and surprise him. I soon saw him – a tall, wiry man with a well-groomed mustache in a business suit. I went toward him smiling. The man I was walking toward saw me approach, took a quick look at me and continued looking out for someone else as if I could not possibly be the person he was waiting for. And maybe he was right. The nameplate he was holding read: "Mr. Gustav van der Kolk."

I began to look at the other nameplates, and I saw my name: Dr. Ile. It couldn't possibly be, I thought, because the hand holding up the nameplate was black. I had spoken to Willem three or four times, and I had never once considered that I was not speaking to a white man. Why had I made that assumption? His accent, diction, syntax, thoughts? I couldn't decide what it was. I had just felt that I knew. I was happy I had only bet against myself, not Ella or Joel. Oh, I wouldn't have heard the last of it.

I approached the man holding the nameplate – a middle-aged, medium-built fellow in a gray shirt and black fedora. That was another thing, I thought. Willem of "Kirk and Klaus" had not sounded like a man who wore a fedora. He had not sounded like a man who wore any kind of cap, but I wouldn't have been too surprised to see him in a bowler hat.

"Hello, I'm Ile," I introduced myself and held out a hand.

The fellow looked at me with a bit of surprise and appeared to hesitate briefly before shaking my hand. I had not expected an embrace, although I wouldn't have been shocked, but the reception was rather cool. What was wrong? Did I not match his own expectations? But how could that be? He already knew my grandfather, and people who knew him said I looked like him. I had expected that he would recognize me before I figured out who he was.

"Are you Mr Willem?" I asked.

"Oh no, I'm a cabdriver; they asked me to pick you up."

I heaved a sigh of relief. So, I hadn't been wrong after all.

"But Willem said he would pick me up himself."

"I don't know. Maybe you should call him."

I did. I got through to Liz, Willem's secretary. She explained that an emergency had come up at the last minute. Willem was currently in a meeting, but he had left a message of welcome. The cab driver was to drive me to their office in Stellenbosch.

"Is Willem OK?" I asked. An emergency always made me think of an ambulance and someone lying unconscious in a hospital bed.

"Yes, he is. Why do you ask?"

"You said there was an emergency."

"Oh no, it's not a medical emergency. It's a...what do you call it...a legal emergency."

"Oh, OK." What on earth was a 'legal emergency'? I wondered. Someone on death row needed Kirk and Klaus to save him, and they had only half an hour to do so? I could almost hear Ella telling me, "Stop overthinking it, Ile."

I turned back to the cabdriver. "What's your name?" I asked. I wasn't sure if we had started off on the right or wrong foot, and I wanted to establish friendly relations as clearly and as quickly as I could. "Mine is Ile," I said, before I realized I was telling him something he already knew.

"I know. My name is Isaac. Welcome to Cape Town," he said as if he was reciting from a manual. "I'll be your driver on our trip to Stellenbosch."

He grabbed my luggage. "It's my job," he told me when I thanked him but asked him not to bother.

"Cape Town is one of the finest cities in South Africa," Isaac said like a tour guide as we drove out of the airport. "It's our Mother City."

It's our Mother City. What or who determined that? I wondered.

"We'll drive through Cape Town on our way to Stellenbosch. Stellenbosch is our Second City. The name means the village of oaks or Eikestad in Afrikaans."

So, my trip was from a first to a second city, a pioneer trail? Was that why my grandfather came here? Or had he simply opened his atlas, spun around, and put a finger on a map as usual? And that map had somehow opened to "Stellenbosch," a place I had not seen in any of the maps of the world I had looked at. But if my grandfather's atlas was as big as Uncle Ibe remembered it, then maybe it contained all types of maps, including a continental map of Africa and perhaps even regional maps.

Isaac seemed to have nothing more to say to me. I concentrated for some time on looking out the window. Cape Town was a stylish city where two oceans converged, a charming metropolis framed by spectacular mountains. Some of the sights were so breathtaking that I told myself I must return one day and explore them with Ella.

"Are there many Nigerians in South Africa?" I asked Isaac. "I mean, Cape Town and Stellenbosch."

"Yes," he answered curtly as if he would rather not discuss the subject.

I was in the mood to talk. I had come a long way to learn everything that I could from everyone possible.

"'Yes' means 'a few' or 'very many'?" I asked.

"Many," he said.

"Do you know any of them?"

"No." Then he seemed to change his mind. "Yes." And to change it again. "Not sure."

"What's the problem, Isaac? Am I bothering you or are Nigerians here troublesome?"

"You're coming from Lagos?" he asked me.

"Yeah."

"So, you're Nigerian?"

"Yes, I am."

"But they told me you're American."

"I'm Nigerian, but I live in America." Was it the custom, I wondered, to tell cab drivers the nationality of their passengers? And how – or why – had anyone come to the conclusion that I was American?

"No wonder," Isaac said. "You sound like a gentleman. The Nigerians here are different."

According to Isaac, Nigerians in South Africa tended to be drug pushers, pimps, prostitutes, grifters, and armed robbers. They loved the "bling lifestyle" – "flashy clothes and jewelry, expensive cars, big houses, even when you can't see how they're making the money" – and they were "messing up" an otherwise well-ordered country. They also tended to lust after South African women.

"You see, our women are beautiful, succulent. Nigerian women are hard, like iron. So, Nigerian men now run after South African women."

"Why is that a problem?" I asked.

"Because they're confusing our women with money and nonsense. These days, you see South African women selling their bodies or even doing drugs. We didn't have any of that before."

"And Nigerians changed everything?"

"Yes. They're confusing our women, and their own women are fighting back because they feel rejected. It's like war."

I looked outside the window. We were traveling across verdant vineyards with rows of ridges that looked like festal braids and somehow spoke to me of smoky mornings and open pastures.

"Where's all this happening – Cape Town or Stellenbosch?"

"No, Stellenbosch is quiet. Only a few Nigerians there. Cape Town, not too many Nigerians. But Jo'berg, that's where you have lots of Nigerians, lots of trouble. I used to live there before I moved to Stellenbosch. If you go to Hillbrow in Jo'berg, it's like you're in Nigeria. They can shoot you for putting your hands in your pocket because they think maybe you have some money.

Some of these Nigerians are so rough and tough they can kill you with bare hands."

"Only Nigerians or other Africans too?"

"There're other Africans in Jo'berg and Cape Town who also cause problems. The Zimbabweans and Mozambicans think they're better than us, yet they're here hustling. But Nigerians are particularly loud, greedy, and arrogant. They shoot themselves too and use their juju against themselves. It's like in the Nigerian movies."

"You watch Nigerian movies?"

"I do, and I see these Nigerians are the same in Nigeria, not just in South Africa."

Beneath the drama that Isaac saw in Nigerian movies, he also discerned a picture of Nigeria that he believed to be real.

"There are four actors," he told me, "they're the biggest actors and actresses in Nigerian movies. Just watch them. They're always cast in the same roles. That tells you everything."

What that told Isaac was that these actors and actresses were not acting at all; they kept appearing in the same roles because that was the way they really were. Nothing I said about verisimilitude and the principles of acting impressed Isaac.

"You can't convince me that someone can be so good in these roles in movie after movie if the person isn't indeed like that."

The other thing he said he learned from watching these movies was that these four roles summed up Nigeria, otherwise why did they keep recurring?

"One is always a wicked witch, the other an evil king, the third will do anything for money, anything, and the fourth is always a wise fool. That's all."

I knew that nothing I said would dissuade Isaac from his point of view. I did not doubt that there were Nigerian criminals in South Africa, but I doubted they were criminals because they were Nigerians. And I knew there must be many other Nigerians who did not fit Isaac's description.

"Do you think that if you expelled every Nigerian immigrant from South Africa your lives would be better?" I asked Isaac.

"Sure. When these Nigerians are not confusing our women, they're taking our places."

"Nigerians are also preventing black South Africans from advancing?"

"Exactly."

"How?"

"They're taking positions meant for black South Africans."

"Be careful of the easy answer," I told him. "In the end, it could cause more harm."

"You don't understand."

Of course, I did not understand. I had seen a video clip of the public execution of a Nigerian immigrant. A group of South African blacks had cornered a young Nigerian boy – he looked as if he was maybe fifteen years old – and they had emptied their guns into him because they wanted to see him "dance." The shooting had produced spasmodic movements even after the boy was apparently dead. And his killers had laughed at "how well he danced." Then they had produced heavy sticks and pounded the corpse until it was merely a smattering of pulp on an otherwise clean city street. What on earth could anyone have done to deserve such a fate? I asked. What chance did the victim have of escaping that fate? If Isaac and his likes were to be believed, he never stood a chance because he committed an Original Sin the moment he arrived in South Africa – the sin of being Nigerian, African, black.

Isaac's outbursts seemed to have put him in a calmer mood. As we entered Stellenbosch, he pointed across the bridge toward a shanty town airing its rusty roofs and ramshackle houses like soiled underwear and said "Kayamandi. That's where I live."

"What's this?" I asked, surprised. "I mean, where's this?"

"Kayamandi. It's a township."

"There are still townships in South Africa?"

"Lots of them."

"And people still live in them?"

He did not consider that question worthy of a response. "You don't understand," I began to say, but I stopped myself in time. I wondered: How on earth could anyone live in such a place beside perhaps some of the finest sceneries anywhere in the world? How could Isaac live in this place, get up in the morning and drive across those vineyards to the Cape Town airport, then drive back again and return to one of these hovels? Was that why he was so angry? What would I do in his stead?

Stellenbosch looked like an engraved chapter from a fairytale. It was so picturesque that it was as if we had stepped away from the real world into a picture-book "village of the oaks" where people could only live happily ever after. Almost every building was painted white. The row of white or whitish buildings, each one detailed in a way that made it unique but still part of an overall pattern, created a surreal effect. The street seemed sedate and people strolled about as if everything was as it should be. But there were also enough runners and bikers to give the impression that this was a fitness town where people were concerned about the shape of their muscles as well as longevity. How had Isaac described it? "Our Second City." But it did not look like a city. It looked like a village that could have become a city but which had instead proudly – and perhaps wisely – chosen not to.

Isaac stopped the car in front of a two-story building with a simple sign: "Kirk and Klaus. Lawyers." He wanted to help me wheel my luggage inside the building, but I assured him there was no need. We shook hands and parted.

Liz welcomed me as if I were an old friend. She had bright eyes and an easy smile, just the way I had imagined. "Oh, I'm so sorry about your grandfather. We all loved him. Willem said to let him know the moment you arrived."

"He's still dealing with the emergency?"

"Yes, but he'll be out in a minute to see you."

Was my grandfather an important client or did they truly love him? Why had he even needed an attorney? Was he someone who liked to utilize the services of attorneys or was there another side of him that was yet to be revealed or that I was still to comprehend?

Willem came out shortly. He was a lean man with a springy walk and a surfeit of vitality. He sounded measured on the phone, but he was a man of such effusive energy that he brushed aside the hand I proffered for a handshake and embraced me warmly instead.

"Very good to see you," he said. "Very good."

He asked about my flight and apologized that he had been unable to pick me up at the airport. Something had come up that he had to resolve personally.

"If you can give me a few more minutes, I should be done, and then we can talk."

He asked Liz to take good care of me meanwhile, made a gesture with his hands to indicate that he would soon return, then he hurried out.

"What can I get for you?" Liz asked me. "Tea, coffee, juice..."

"I'll take a walk instead."

"A walk?"

I explained that I'd rather take a walk around the block and see a bit more of the town. Hopefully, by the time I returned Willem would have finished dealing with the legal emergency.

She gave me a street map and marked where the office was. "If you have any problem, just walk back to this point."

"I don't intend to go far. In fact, I probably won't go beyond any point where I can no longer see this office."

"That's a good plan."

I didn't intend to take a long walk, but there was something seductive about Stellenbosch. Every building was so unique, every tree so old that my short walk soon became longish. Could anywhere be this perfect? No, I'll walk around until I found a house that wasn't white or whitish or an oak tree that wasn't a champion tree. I must have walked quite a few blocks and made some turns before I decided I had to suspend my search for the time being, at least while I could still make my way back without too many inquiries. Besides, I had also become aware of something odd. I was in front of the four columns of the majestic Town Hall looking at a painting of Nelson Mandela as well as an apparently homeless black man sleeping on a nearby bench when it struck me that virtually everyone I had seen in this fabled Second City was white. I could as well have been walking down the street somewhere in Europe. In some parts of Europe, I would have seen more blacks already.

At the beginning of my walk, I had seen two young women walking on the other side of the road. As I passed them, I heard one use the phrase "social constructivism" in a sentence. I stopped to take a good look at them and to reflect: In what sort of town do two young women – one with the figure of a model and the other quite voluptuous – have a conversation about social constructivism as they walked down the street? This must be a marvelous town indeed. About half an hour later, in front of the Town Hall, I reflected instead on what Uncle Ibe had once said to me: "Some people say if something is too good to be true, you should be careful. I say if something is too good to be true, you should run. Fast." Running was out of it, I decided, but there was something not right here. Just a few minutes away was a township teeming with blacks and here was an idyllic town where nearly everyone I could see strolling about was white. Where had my grandfather lived – in the township?

I returned to Kirk and Klaus. Willem was waiting for me

in his office. I felt like I already knew him.

"You said you'd tell me when I got here," I reminded him. "How did my grandfather die?"

"He went to bed and did not wake up."

Just like my father. "Was he sick?" I asked.

"Not really."

"What happened?"

"That's it. He went to bed and didn't wake up. The maid discovered him when she arrived in the morning to clean the house. I spoke with him the previous day and he didn't complain about anything."

"Tell me about him."

"As I've said before, your grandfather was unique. If he had told me that he fell from the sky and was the son of heaven or something like that, I wouldn't have doubted him."

"Why?"

"It was the way he was, the way he carried himself, the way nobody knew anything about him. I'm not quite sure why. So, when he told me he wanted to bequeath everything he had to his grandson, I was surprised but not too much."

"How did he know about me?"

"I don't know, but I'll take you to his house, your house now. Maybe you can piece these things together from there."

"How did you become his attorney?"

"He walked in one day and retained us to do what lawyers do for privileged clients and to manage his affairs at a time like this."

I couldn't see my grandfather – that is, his corpse – because he had already been buried. Willem said they waited three months after his death because they were determined to find me, but that had proved impossible then.

"My grandfather bequeathed his wealth to me. What does that mean?"

"He left his house and everything in it, the money in his bank account here, and an investment account in London."

"London?"

"Yes. Apparently, he bought a pools ticket while he was a student there and won the jackpot. He invested the money well."

Was that where the money for the hospital and King Lazarus came from? But...pools betting? That didn't sound like my grandfather. Or maybe it did.

"Are you sure?" I asked.

"Not one hundred percent, but we believe that's what happened."

"Where did he come from to Stellenbosch, or has he been here for forty-four years?"

"No, he came here three years ago and I think he recently started making plans to leave next year."

"He only planned to live here for four years?"

"That's what it looks like."

"Where did he come from?"

"I don't know."

"Where was he planning to go to?"

"I don't know."

Had my grandfather been wandering the world since 1974, stopping at a place for only three or four years? Was he still a priest in his mind even if he was never named one in reality? Four was the sign of the crossroads as well as the marketplace. We had only four market days. Or was there something else going on here? What was I to do next – go home from Stellenbosch as planned or start retracing my grandfather's footsteps? Was this why everyone else had preferred "not to dig up old graves," as my aunt phrased it?

"When are you going to take me to the house?" I asked Willem.

"Whenever you're ready."

The house was a gated white building with intricate patterns that Willem said was typical of Cape Dutch architecture and so much glassy exterior – glass doors, glass windows, a glassy veranda – that it glittered. It was not the sort of house I had expected my grandfather to own, unless of course he had chosen it the way he chose almost everything – with an unseeing finger. Or maybe he had bought it because of the champion trees, which formed a grove of antiquity that cusped the house's radiant claim to modernity in parenthesis.

"Did my grandfather choose this house?" I asked Willem.

The question seemed to puzzle him. "He must have," he said slowly. "He lived here."

"No, what I mean is did he see this house before buying it?"

"I don't know. We had nothing to do with the purchase, but he didn't complain about the house."

I almost wanted to ask if my grandfather had planted the trees, but that would have been ridiculous. The trees were so old that they were probably there when the pioneers trudged up the hill, or sauntered down the hill, to found a new settlement. It was a sobering thought. These trees must have witnessed so much more history than myself, so much more history than any human being alive. But they were mute. I wondered: What happens to a history that is muted? Is it fated to stand like these ageless trees with voiceless revelations?

Willem opened the door, handed me the key, and said he needed to get back to the office. "We'll talk after you're done here and sign the necessary documents tomorrow. I'll pick you up for dinner later, if that's OK."

"Of course. I don't know anywhere here."

"In that case, I'll take you to somewhere special." He laughed as if he couldn't wait to surprise me with the sort of culinary indulgence that he had in mind.

"Thanks, Willem. I'll be waiting."

The interior of the house was mostly a large living room and three bedrooms. The living room wasn't really a place to receive visitors or to watch television or something of the sort. It was a gallery. The white walls were covered with pictures, drawings, paintings, writings, and other artifacts. It was an assemblage that I assumed told a story, but everything wasn't arranged according to a clear pattern. There was a picture of my grandmother. Beneath it was a strip of paper on which was written, in my grandfather's scrawly handwriting: "Goddess of the morning." The other pictures and drawings were mostly of family members and friends – my father, mother, Uncle Ibe, Aunt Rosette, myself, Egwuatu – and some other people that I didn't know or couldn't recognize. How on earth did my picture get there? I knew that picture. It was the same one on my university web page. How had my grandfather known who I was or that I existed? There was also a picture of King Lazarus when it still shone with new paint after it had just been built. And there was a picture of a white woman with blonde hair, a shy smile, and a wistful look. Behind her was an elaborate sunset that looked like an explosion of colors. Was that real? Beneath the picture was the line: "How she loved sunsets!" Was that Ann Pottinger? Who was she? What did she mean to my grandfather?

Besides the pictures, there were paintings of people that looked like landscapes or landscapes that looked like people. Was that Uncle Ibe? Was that me? Who were these people? Where were these places? And who was the painter? On one end of the long room was a canvas on an easel that sort of answered my question. My grandfather must have learned to paint. But even if he did, how could he paint this well?

As I looked at the pictures, drawings, and paintings, it dawned on me that I now had to accept the thought I had been resisting – that my grandfather had walked out on his family to live another life elsewhere. I still didn't know why. But was there any reason that would explain a man leaving three young children to fend for themselves, even if he bequeathed his wealth to them? Did he leave because of Ann Pottinger? What sort of man would that make him? What was I to think of such a man? But I told myself to calm down. The pictures only told half the tale, or even less.

There were other artifacts on that wall. There was a wood carving with a head, or the idea of a head, on one end. Uncle Ibe had once told me that the symbol of the earth goddess was "a symbol with a head." Was this it? If it was, how did my grandfather get it and what was it doing on his wall? There was a rosary, the largest I had ever seen, mounted in such a way that it formed a triangle. Why the triangle? I wondered. There were paintings of such horrific scenes – a tidal wave sweeping away houses, people that looked like skeletons, hospitals or what looked like hospitals overflowing with patients like debris in muddy water – that I opted not to unravel what they referred to. And then there were paintings of such idyllic scenes – explosive sunsets, a shimmering sunrise, a view of a mountain that looked like a table and appeared to have risen out of a surfing sea.

There were also playbills on that wall. Had my grandfather been to see these musicals – *Carmen*, *King Kong*, and *Pippin* – or had he merely collected the posters? There was something rather jarring about these musicals. In *Carmen* and *King Kong*, the lover ends up killing the beloved. Why would that interest my grandfather? But then there was *Pippin*. Beneath the poster, my grandfather had copied and pasted the quote: "I believe if I refuse to grow old, I can stay young 'til I die." Had he believed that? What was his fascination with musicals? There was a story here, several stories, but I didn't know what it was or how they were all related. Perhaps, I told myself, I had embarked on a quest where I was likely to end up knowing less than what actually happened.

One of the bedrooms was evidently unused. It had a bed, a night table, and the usual bedroom furniture. But there didn't seem to be any personal item there that belonged to my grandfather or anybody else. Did he ever have guests? Maybe not. I had reasoned that everything on the wall in the living room must be important and must have been put up there for a reason. So, I concluded that this room wasn't particularly important to my quest.

The other bedroom was furnished in the same fashion, but it seemed to have been used. There was no personal item in it, yet I had the feeling that it had been used. Why did that feeling persist? Was the room simply musty or was there another kind of smell that I almost recognized but could not name? But my grandfather had been dead for more than four months, so maybe it was my imagination that was dancing around inside my head.

The next room must have been my grandfather's. It had clothes and other items that I believed were his. When I opened the drawer of the night table, it was there waiting for me – the atlas I had heard so much about. There was a strip of paper pasted on the front, and on it was clearly written: "For Ile." My grandfather had actually written my name: F-o-r I-l-e. He must have spoken it too. And thought it. It was also his name after all. There were, again, so many questions swirling in my head, but I simply opened the atlas. Uncle Ibe was right. On the inside front cover was scrawled the sentence: "A man will set forth." There was another sentence beneath it: "A man set forth." One was a proposal, the other its accomplishment. I flipped through the atlas hoping to find some signs that whispered what had happened in the last forty-four years, but almost all the pages looked the same – worn, as if they had been thumbed too many times or were aging at the same pace.

On the last page, there were two newspaper clippings. One was about the moon landing in 1969. The other was about an epidemic in 1974, a report reproduced from *The New York Times*: "*At least 10,000—and perhaps as many as 20,000—people in the northeastern Indian state of Bihar have died so far this year from smallpox in what has been described as one of the worst epidemics of the viral disease in recent years.*" What was the connection? I had so many questions that I actually began to scratch my head. A man had walked on the moon and my grandfather, a neighborhood King Lazarus, had set out five years later to save the world or raise the dead or help the afflicted, forsaking his own family? Was that it? Why had he waited five years? How did he go from Fegge to Bihar? Why did he care about what was happening in India? Maybe his disappearance wasn't because of Ann Pottinger, whoever she was. But did that make it any better? I should feel outraged. But...I didn't. Had all the years of admiring my grandfather inoculated me against that sort of outrage? Or did I feel some sympathy for his cause that I dared not admit even to myself? How could anyone tear himself away from the joys and comfort of family to roam the world like an outcast? What difference could one man make? On the inside back cover of the atlas, as if he had anticipated my question, my grandfather had written two sentences. The first was: "I have seen the future, and it is something like the past."

I now had more unanswered questions than I had arrived with. On one corner of the living room was a desk with a laptop on it. I opened it, and I was surprised. For some reason, I sometimes assumed that Uncle Ibe must have taken after my grandfather. But I wasn't sure that Uncle Ibe owned a computer, and he would probably joke that "wifi" must be a new code word for "bush meat." My grandfather owned a laptop. But the computer had nothing to say to me. There were no files that I could read.

The thought occurred to me that if he had worked as a volunteer in disaster areas around the world, he might have registered with an international agency. Fortunately, there was a phone beside the desk. I didn't know if I could make international calls, but I drew up a list of agencies and began calling.

"Hello, my name is Ile, and I'm calling from South Africa. I'm calling to find out if my grandfather was ever a volunteer with your agency at any time in any part of the world."

"That's not the sort of information that we routinely give

out."

"This is no routine. My grandfather recently died, and I'm trying to put his affairs in order. The information will help me make an important determination."

"Your grandfather?"

"Yes."

"What was his name?"

"Ileka. Ile Ka. He sometimes spelt it in different ways."

"You do understand that we may not have a record of every single individual that has worked with us during these difficult times?"

"I do. Thanks for your help."

I called several agencies. None of them had any record of my grandfather. Had he used a pseudonym? But why would he do that? Or had he not volunteered officially? That was the sort of thing I could imagine him doing – just walking in to help out and walking away when he felt he had done all he could. And then moving on to the next apocalypse. What had he done in between disasters?

I wasn't sure what to do next. My grandfather was a doctor, so maybe he would have worked with other doctors in disaster areas. I called Doctors without Borders again. I had called them before to ask if they had any record of my grandfather. The person I spoke with had asked me to repeat the name. Twice. I called them now to ask if they could direct me to someone who had worked in several disaster areas. The operator asked me to repeat my grandfather's name again, then she said "There's someone here who wants to speak with you. He was here when you called the last time."

The person I spoke with introduced himself as Ivan, "a doctor and a free agent," and asked me to describe my grandfather. It struck me as rather odd that I could describe a man I never met better than some of the people I knew.

"He's from Nigeria, he's big, and he has a furrow across his forehead?"

"Yes."

"He walks with a bit of a limp?"

I didn't know about the limp.

Ivan apparently took my silence as confirmation. "And he's a rainmaker, a real rainmaker?"

How many rainmakers, "real rainmakers," could there be in the world who fit that description?

"Yes. How did you know that?"

"You're talking about Aileek..."

"Ileka. Ile Ka."

"That's the name. Unbelievable. And you're his grandson? I didn't know he had any family. He never talked about himself."

"How did you know he was a rainmaker?"

"Because I saw him make rain in Ethiopia. I was there during that terrible drought. There was no water because the rain only fell grudgingly – if at all – and the government was making things harder. The farms had dried up, so there was a massive famine. Then Aileek arrived one night and went out into one of the farms and called down the rain. It rained for one night and one day. It rained so much that the farm was flooded. This is a true story, believe me. We watched as he whispered into his cupped hands, then gestured to the air. The rain fell for some time, then he did it all over again. Until then, I thought that rainmaking was one more fable out of Africa. After that night, I could never forget him."

"Did he stop the drought?"

"He did a lot of good, saved a lot of lives. He did more than his share, if you ask me. But he couldn't keep making rain because every time he did we could see that it took something out of him. It was like a sacrifice."

"Did you see him again after that night, I mean after Ethiopia?"

"I saw him almost everywhere I went after that, every disaster area. We became friendly toward each other. Every time I saw him, I would ask him or he would ask me: 'Are you following me or am I following you?' He never talked about his family, so I assumed he had none. He was a remarkable man, and I'm not just saying that for the sake of it."

"When was the last time you saw him?"

"I remember, because I kind of missed seeing him after that. The last time I saw him was in Banda Aceh."

"The Indian Ocean tsunami?"

"Yes, he was there. But something bad happened to him because he had to be carried out. I never saw him after that. Where's he now?"

"He's dead."

The phone fell silent.

"Hello..."

"I'm still here," Ivan said in a tired voice. "It's kind of sad. Aileek saved many many lives. I saw him raise a man from the dead in Bangladesh."

"He did what?"

"It was a horrible cyclone, and there were several thousands dead. As it turned out, this man wasn't actually dead, but he would have died for sure if Aileek hadn't saved him. Listen: If there's ever any way I can help you out with anything, or even just to talk, please call me."

I thanked him. My grandfather had obviously made a difference in the world. But couldn't he have done it some other way? I couldn't get past the fact that he had walked out on my father and his siblings – and when they were still so young. Had he planned to return? Why hadn't he? The only thing that was certain was that he had walked out on his family and spent thirty years of his life going from one disaster area to another; he had stopped when he was already seventy-four years old and perhaps because "something bad" happened to him after a tsunami. He had had to be carried out, but he must have recovered and somehow ended up in Stellenbosch. Where had he been in the intervening years? The more I drank the more I thirsted.

My mind returned to that picture of a blonde woman on the wall, the one who loved sunsets. Was that Ann Pottinger? Who was Ann Pottinger? Perhaps it was not impossible to find out, I thought. I might get lucky again. I went online and searched for "Ann Pottinger, London, phone number." I made a list, then I started calling. But I still couldn't find her, and it was not for want of trying.

I went back to the wall and began studying the assemblage again. On the upper part of the wall and through parts of the montage were marks that I had interpreted before as simply textural. But the more I studied them, the more they looked like raindrops. Were they? Had my grandfather's last act as a rainmaker been right here on this wall? Was this the morning dew? As my uncle sometimes said, "The morning dew may not be rain but it wets the grass too."

I called Uncle Ibe.

"How are you, Ile? I used to call you Americana. What do I call you now?"

"Never mind, uncle. I have a quick question."

"Why 'quick'? You haven't heard that there's no hurry in life?"

"True, but I have a meeting soon."

"OK, ask."

"What precisely does the symbol of the earth goddess look like?"

"Why do you ask?"

"I'm looking at a painting, and I'm wondering if the artist got the details right."

"You've always been smart, Ile. I'll believe you for now

because I know that one day you'll tell me the truth."

As he described the symbol, the details corresponded to the features of the carving in front of me. Was it an original or a replica that my grandfather made? I couldn't ask Uncle Ibe any further questions. He often joked about things, but he had a sharp mind.

"Thanks, uncle," I told him. "This painting is way off."

"Be careful of bogus things."

"The best way to see Stellenbosch is to walk," Willem told me. He had arrived to take me out to dinner without his car. It was a fairly small town, and he had already told me that I was right in the center, close to the Botanical Garden, so walking should not be arduous. But I had to slow him down from time to time because he tended to walk at a fast pace as if he was late for a business meeting or had another emergency to hurry toward. It felt a bit strange locking up my grandfather's house, mine according to Willem, as if I had always lived there.

The dinner was sumptuous. Willem ordered two platters of several South African dishes that reminded me of the sort of spread we had been welcomed with at Nathan's. I ate heartily.

"If I want to order this again, I mean another time, what should I ask for?" I asked Willem. He had made the order in Afrikaans.

"Just come to this same place and ask for a special braai platter."

"Not just any braai platter?"

"No, this is the special platter. It's only for extra special guests."

"In that case, it should be the 'extra special platter.'"

We both laughed.

"There are many restaurants and bars in this town, more restaurants and bars than I've seen in many towns this size," I said.

"And they're all teeming with patrons. What's the secret?"

"It's a campus town," he said simply. "When the students are on holiday, everything kind of slows down."

"What about tourists?"

"Yes, there are many tourists too, especially those who come to see South Africa's winelands."

"I like you," Willem said after we had chatted for some time. "You're like your grandfather. You speak from the heart."

"But you said my grandfather didn't talk much."

"About himself. He sometimes talked about other things."

"Did he ever mention Ann Pottinger?"

"Not to me."

"Or to anyone else in your firm?"

"Your grandfather only dealt with me. My partner runs our office in Pretoria. Your grandfather never even met him. Who's Ann Pottinger?"

"I don't know, but I'd like to find out."

"Sorry I can't help you there."

"You mentioned a maid that came to clean the house. Who's she? I'd like to talk to her."

"I can arrange a meeting in our office or at your house."

"I'd prefer to go and meet her."

"She lives in the township, Kayamandi. You shouldn't go there."

"Why not?"

"Because it can be dangerous."

"But the township is just across the bridge there. If going there is dangerous, why is it safe for us to sit here wining and dining?"

"You don't understand." Isaac had said the same thing.

"I'd rather go to Kayamandi," I said.

"If you insist."

I went there the next day.

Willem had given me a name and a phone number. I called the number a few times, but no one answered. Kayamandi was a different sort of neighborhood, but it was a suburb of Stellenbosch, so I walked the short distance to the place. The nearer I got the more blacks and coloreds I saw on the streets and the spotless appearance that characterized Stellenbosch began to give way to blemishes – run-down houses, visibly unsanitary conditions, discount and liquor stores alive with poverty and desperation. Right after the entrance to Kayamandi, beside a well-paved road that divided rows of rickety houses that looked as if they had been cobbled together against their will, I stopped a young boy in a bright red shirt and asked him for directions.

"Where are you from?" he asked me.

"Why do you ask?" I queried back. Willem had advised me not to speak to anyone.

"Your accent, it's familiar."

Where was I from? It was no longer a simple question with a simple answer. I wanted to say "America." "I'm Nigerian," I said instead.

"I thought so," he said exultantly. "My best friend is from Nigeria."

"Your best friend is from Nigeria?"

"Yes, his name is Ugo. It means feather."

"I know," I said thoughtfully.

"My name is Louie," he told me. "Who are you looking for? I know everyone in Kayamandi."

"Really? How old are you?"

"Thirteen."

"And you already know everybody?"

"I get around," he said with a wink and a smile.

"I'm looking for Thelma. She's a maid or she used to be a maid for a man who died a few months ago. He was from Nigeria and—"

"You mean Monk?"

"No, Ile Ka."

"That's him. Monk."

"I don't understand. Did you know him? And why do you call him Monk?"

"Or The Monk. He lived like one, and he was a good man. We held a funeral procession for him, a big one. I'll take you to Miss Thelma. Everyone calls her Miss Thelma."

With Louie talking about everything and anything he could think of, we went deeper into the inner city called Kayamandi, or "nice home" in Xhosa. Once upon a time, it had been a settlement for migrant black male laborers working in farms in and around Stellenbosch. The "hostels" had since transformed into a crowded township wrinkled by poverty and neglect.

Thelma's house was not unlike the other dwellings in Kayamandi, but it had a well-carved oak door, the sort to be expected in a mansion. "That's a nice door, isn't it?" Louie asked rhetorically. "We're all proud of it." He bid me goodbye as I knocked on the door.

I expected a question – "Who are you" or "Who are you looking for?" – since Thelma neither knew my identity nor that I was coming to see her. But the plump woman with a kindly face who opened the door stepped back as if she was shocked to see me. The startled look on her face was gradually replaced by one of comprehension, then an expression of joy melted her face as she rushed forward and enfolded me in her arms like a mother welcoming back a long-lost child. She drew back and ululated, beaming.

"I knew you would come," she said.

"You know me?"

"Of course. You look exactly the way he must have when he was younger. I mean Monk."

She almost dragged me inside and sat me down in what appeared to be the most comfortable chair in her cramped living room. I had to dissuade her from bringing food. I had had rooibos tea with some rusks that I discovered in one of the kitchen cabinets that morning, and Willem had invited me to a "business lunch" later in the day.

"Why do you call him Monk? The boy that brought me here, Louie, called him that too. But his attorney in Stellenbosch never mentioned that."

"Mr Willem? Maybe he still will, but people over there didn't know him the way we did. He was Monk not only because he lived like one but because he had a good heart the way a monk should. It was as if he lived for something higher than himself, higher than all of us."

"How long did you know him?"

"Three years. You see, when he first came, he hired a cleaning service and they used to send maids to clean his house. Unfortunately, some of them, or a few of them, stole his sardines."

"Stole his sardines? Is that a metaphor?" I asked her.

"No, your grandfather loved sardines – sardines in olive oil. For some reason, some of the maids would steal sardine cans. They could have asked, but they didn't. So, he said he didn't want any more maids."

My grandfather loved sardines? This must be a recent love, I thought, because no one had ever mentioned that before. In fact, no one had mentioned food in relation to my grandfather before. Why sardines? I wondered.

"Then, one day, he came to Kayamandi. It was early evening, and I was outside when I saw him rush across the street. A car almost knocked him down. I was on the verge of retreating indoors because I thought something was pursuing him. He was in front of me before I knew it, and he hit his forehead as if there was a spirit inside that was threatening to come out. I had never seen anything like that before. But there was something about him that gave off a good aura all the same. 'It is you,' he said in an excited whisper. He offered me a job right there. I told him I already had as many cleaning jobs as I could handle. He waved away my protests and told me he would take care of all that. That was how I went to work for him, only him. As I knew him better, I would have worked for him even without payment."

"What did you do for him?"

"Initially, I cleaned the house, and that was it. He hardly said anything to me. But, gradually, he began to talk to me. He liked to talk sometimes, and he told me so many things. He also used a meal delivery service. After some time, I told him I couldn't let him do that anymore, so I began to cook for him. We became friends, and he started coming here whenever he could. Every time he did, he would ask me to gather everyone I could and he would listen to their problems and help out whenever he could. He would take down their names and then ask them to go see his lawyer, who would know what to do. I tell you, there are many people in this township who got a better start in life or who are alive today because of your grandfather. He kept asking me what he could do for me, and I told him all I wanted was a nice door. He got me that door."

"A door?"

"Yes, a door. It doesn't sound like much, but it means a lot to me. All my life, for fifty-five years, I've lived in townships. My mother still lives in Khayelitsha, and some of my children are in Gugulethu. All we've known, in happiness and in sorrow, are townships. I've cleaned houses until my hands are almost starting to peel. Take a look."

I did. Her wrinkled hands were so mottled that they looked like an old house with faded paint.

"The thing I always dreaded the most was not the cleaning but knocking on that mansion door for the first time, not knowing what lay beyond it. Sometimes, I would whisper to the door as if it was a spirit. 'Please, let the forces beyond be kind.' 'Please, let my fortunes improve or at least remain the same after I cross this threshold.' So, yes, I wanted a mansion door. Your grandfather understood. That was the thing about him. He didn't ask a lot of questions; he understood."

"How did he die?"

"He went to sleep and didn't wake up. The previous evening, he was fine. He was staring at his wall of everything when I left. Sometimes, he could stare at that wall for hours, then he would make one change or the other; the next day, he could reverse the change or make another one. He said it was a work in progress, like our lives. You can imagine my shock when I arrived the next morning and he was dead. Oh, I was so so heartbroken," she said with tears in her eyes. "Sometimes, I still cry when I think about him. I know he was old, but still he was gone too soon. When I came back to Kayamandi with the news, you've never seen so many people weeping.

"The very next Sunday, after church, people simply started lining up as if it was pre-planned. It wasn't. We held a procession for him around Kayamandi, but that was not enough. So, we marched through Stellenbosch to his house and back. We've never done that before, but then we've never had someone like him among us. We sang for him the train song, because we knew he came from somewhere far away. But it didn't matter where he came from. He had become one of us, and it was from here that he took the train to heaven. We sang with all our hearts:

    Shosholoza, shosholoza
    Ku lezontaba
    Stimela sphume South Africa
    Wen' uyabaleka
    Wen' uyabaleka
    Ku lezontaba

> Stimela siphume South Africa

Our song wasn't really about death. It was about parting and moving, how the destination is always ahead until we die, how life is sweet one moment and bitter the next, how we may never understand much of it but we have to keep moving because that's the rhythm of life.

"We sang other songs, and I sang for him with all my soul:
> Senzeni na?
>
> Sono sethu, ubumnyama?
>
> Sono sethu yinyaniso?
>
> Sibulawayo
>
> Mayibuye i Africa

"That was a song of desolation, of the oncoming redemption. He went everywhere that he could and did everything possible to transform the desolation of the human spirit. It didn't matter where it was or who was affected – black, white, yellow, brown, red, green. The only thing that mattered to him was that he was needed. He didn't know our sorrow before he arrived here, but he already carried it with him. I wish I had enough words to talk about him, but he was ngaphaya kwamagama. Your grandfather was a man among men, a monk. You should be proud of him."

She took some time to wipe the tears streaking down her face and recompose herself. It felt as if she was mourning someone she had known all her life.

"I saw him angry only once in all those years," she told me.

"When?"

"He was listening to the radio and he heard someone describe apartheid as 'affirmative action for Afrikaners.' He was so angry that he saw stars, he said. His whole body vibrated, but he calmed himself. He said the sad thing about history is that it's everybody's prostitute."

"He did?"

"I never heard him use that type of language before or after."

"He saw stars." "He vibrated." Was my grandfather also afflicted with my type of anger disorder? But this was the first time I ever heard anyone mention that he lost his temper. He was legendary for maintaining his temper even in the most stressful situations.

"Did he tell you about his previous life in Nigeria?"

"He sometimes mentioned 'a previous lifetime,' but it was one of the things that he didn't want to talk about. I always felt that something bad happened back then. But he talked about you sometimes, your progress."

"How did he know about me?"

"He never said. Your grandfather was one of those people that I'm not sure it's possible to ever quite understand in that way. He was a man who sometimes seemed to push himself too hard, but he was a priceless light in a world of darkness. He was umfundisi."

"What's that?"

"A priest."

"Did he tell you about his village?"

"No, he didn't talk about that."

"Did he ever mention Ann Pottinger?"

"Who's she?"

"I believe her picture is on his wall, the one with a colorful sunset."

"No, he didn't talk about her. He didn't talk about this either, but he gave it to me the week before he died."

She pointed to a painting on the wall behind her. It was in the style of the other paintings on my grandfather's wall. In the painting, someone was being dug out from a heap of debris. Was that what happened to my grandfather in Banda Aceh? Was he the person in the picture? Who were the people doing the digging?

And why did he give this painting to Thelma?

"Did he tell you why he gave you this painting?" I asked her.

"To thank me for everything I did for him. That's what he said. I told him I was the one who should be thanking him."

"He thanked you for your services the week before his death?"

"So it turned out."

It dawned on me anew that there was something, maybe some things, about my grandfather that I would never understand even if I trailed him to the end of the earth.

The thinning road that I had been following finally disappeared altogether. In its place was a forest that seemed as if it had been there from the beginning of the world. The person I had asked for directions had told me that the only way to the village was through this forest.

"There is no other way?"

"None."

"Has anyone ever traveled through this forest?"

"No one can pass through it. It's impenetrable."

I understood forests and I knew my way through them, but it seemed incredible that the patient had somehow managed to travel for days through this forest to get to the clinic where he died. He had told the men who brought him in that the demon was after him, but what sort of demon could make a man travel through an impenetrable forest to get to a clinic when it was possibly evident to him that he was already beyond salvation? Or was he seeking help for others as afflicted as he was?

It all started some days ago when I was called back to the clinic because of an emergency. In the small town in which the clinic was located, telephone services were unreliable, so emergency calls often had to be made by sending an attendant to summon a doctor. There were only two doctors, the medical director and myself, so emergency calls had more or less become routine. It was a poor province, and people sometimes waited to go to the clinic only when their illness indeed required immediate attention. Many of them preferred to consult a herbalist first, so going to the clinic was deferred until – or if – the herbalist was unable to heal them. I suggested to the medical director that we could also provide "herbal healing."

"You can't be serious," he said. "You want us to turn this clinic into a herbal home?"

"No, not turn it into a herbal home. We can add alternative medicine, as much as possible, to the treatments we already provide."

"You want us to employ a herbalist here?"

"No, I know enough to provide that service."

"You? You're a trained medical doctor, aren't you?"

"You know I am."

"Then what are you talking about? Where did you even learn herbal healing?"

"In a previous lifetime."

"What does that mean?"

I was only passing through and volunteering at this provincial clinic. I decided that I would keep doing so, but I also began providing herbal treatment in the evenings at a herbal home that I provisioned. Because I couldn't work without ceasing and because of the constant emergency calls, I employed a herbalist, Mama Yaa, to assist me there. She would take over the herbal home whenever I left.

Mama Yaa was a popular healer in the province. People came from so many places to see her. She wasn't the only healer around. Herbal healing was a common practice, something that it seemed anyone who could tell the difference between two different kinds of plants ventured into. But Mama Yaa had a reputation for actually healing people. And she did not do so, or fail to do so, after making the sick to dance until they were almost lame or sacrificing chickens that could have been spared for the soup pot. She listened to people's complaints, examined them, and then recommended or gave them herbs that often helped them get better. She was a slim, middle-aged woman who favored a peculiar headdress that some people said was a magical accessory. She had become known as Mama Yaa because she had a habit of saying "Yaa" or "Yes, yaa" as she listened to her patients to encourage them to speak more. She also tended to exhale "Yaa" as she went through the process of healing as if to assure everyone that everything was indeed going the way it should.

When I told the medical director that I could heal with herbs, I was relying on knowledge that I had gained, and incompletely so, a long time ago. I could indeed heal certain illnesses with herbs, but Mama Yaa's knowledge in this regard was superior to mine. So, I told her I would provide whatever she needed to improve her work if she would partner with me.

When that emergency call came, I was at the herbal home. I entrusted the place to Mama Yaa and rushed to the clinic. A man had been brought in; he was barely conscious. He was so emaciated that his ribs were quite evident. He was coughing blood and had a very high temperature. The two men who had brought him in said they had found him where he had collapsed on the side of the road and did not know anything about him. The patient was determined to say something, and we could see him struggling to get the words out. Eventually, he was able to utter only a single word before he died. I asked the men what the word meant, and they shook their heads to indicate they didn't know. They only remembered the man muttering that the demon was after him when they picked him up.

"But that single word must have been so important that he struggled with everything he had just to say it. Is there any way we can find out what it means?"

They shook their heads again.

I decided that I must find out. Fortunately, one of the nurses was able to identify that word as the name of a village that lay beyond the forest. One of the men then said that he had heard that "story" before. I didn't want to question him about why he did not say so the first time. I wondered: If the village was indeed as they described it, how could this man have made the journey in his state? Or had his condition deteriorated rapidly after he set out?

"We must get to the root of this," I said to the medical director.

"But the man is already dead."

He was a good doctor, but he was not an epidemiologist.

"That's not what I mean. This man walked through the forest with debilitating symptoms only to die before he could be treated. We need to take his blood sample and send it out for testing. Meanwhile, we should quarantine everyone who came into contact with him. Until we know what his ailment was, we should take precautions."

"We don't want to alarm anyone. This is an isolated case."

"We don't know that. It's a public health issue until we can prove otherwise."

"But you also came into contact with him."

"Yes, I'll go into quarantine with the two men and the nurse."

"Quarantine? We don't have the facility."

"We do – in the herbal home."

"You quarantine people there?"

"We've never done that, but we can do so if necessary."

"I thought you said you were passing through?"

"I'm always passing through, but that's no reason not to do what I can."

I convinced the men that brought in the patient and the nurse that attended to him to go into quarantine with me. By the third day, all three were gravely ill. By the end of the week, they were all dead.

"I don't know what we're dealing with," I told the medical director, "so I have to go to the source to find out. That's the only way we can stop it. That's probably why the patient made that impossible journey. He realized that whatever it was needed the sort of intervention that was beyond the resources in his village."

"You want to go to the source, the very place that someone or maybe several people are fleeing from?"

"It's my calling."

"Your calling? Everyone else who came into contact with the patient died, except you. What's the medical explanation for that?"

"Not everything can be explained."

I didn't want to go into the story of how I found out about myself, about my immunity to a disease that killed nearly everyone in its path. When I realized this about myself, I decided that the course of my life was set. I did not understand the logic or extent of my immunity, so I always assumed that going toward the source of any epidemic was a journey toward death. But I could not imagine staying back because of that.

That was how I set off for the village beyond the forest. As I traveled deeper and deeper into the forest, I understood why people were terrified of forests. They were lonely places where even silence echoed and there was no telling what lay in wait beyond the next tree or clump of bushes. What if a wild animal suddenly appeared? What if a spirit suddenly called? But I was used to forests. I had lived in them so many times that they had become like homes to me. Sometimes, when I was passing through a village, I made my home in the nearest forest. I considered them safe and serene; they were ideal for meditation. But I was in a hurry. My movement was made difficult because I was carrying my emergency response kit.

This forest was thicker than many others I've been in. It looked untraveled as if nothing had passed through since the very beginning. Perhaps there weren't many hunters and trappers in this province, I thought. Maybe there was no ogba ngbada or its likes, not only to tame the forest but also to foster brotherhood. How then had the patient been able to accomplish the impossible feat of traveling through this forest? In my village, that would have made him an ogba ngbada. The final test before initiation into the brotherhood was to spend a whole market week, four days, living and traveling through the forest.

I kept moving, telling the time where possible by slivers of sunlight that penetrated through the tall trees. As I went deeper, the trees became thicker until I was traveling between trees that sometimes looked like four or more gigantic dancers wrapped together. This must be the heart of the forest. I kept moving, sometimes humming a song to urge myself on. I had a destination that no one seemed to have actually seen, but I was determined to get there. This forest was a natural buffer between the village beyond and the small town that I was coming from, but it was only a matter of time before other patients – if they were desperate enough – began to come through it. Desperation also awakens imagination. The big trees finally began to give way to medium-sized ones, and I sensed that I was getting close to the village.

And there it lay – a village of mud houses with thatched roofs. I had traveled for three days, I think, to get there. There were burning fires around the village "to drive away evil spirits," I was told, and a barricade at the entrance that regulated movement. But all these were farther from view. In front of me was a long, open hut that I assumed must be some sort of religious place because of the cross in front of it; beside it was another hut that looked like a home. In front of the first hut were fresh graves on which crosses made of twigs had been planted. A white woman in a habit stood in this desolate graveyard crying and praying. When I emerged from the forest, she promptly took to her heels. I had to entreat her to come back.

"Who are you, and how did you get here?" she asked with trepidation when she finally returned.

It took some time to calm her down and explain my mission. There were four of them, she told me, and their mission was to "bring the gospel" to this village beyond the forest.

"How did you get here?" I asked her.

"Our mission is to spread the gospel to forgotten places in remote regions of the world."

She showed me a clearing. A helicopter had airlifted them from the small town that I was coming from and brought them there. The same helicopter came every other month to bring supplies. But, in between the visits, some sort of epidemic broke out in the village and it had already killed several villagers and three missionaries. She expected that she too would soon die.

"Why would you come here now?" she asked me.

"This is when I'm needed here. I need to get to the village."

"If you cross that line," she said, pointing to an invisible line between the graveyard and the village, "you'll surely die."

"But if I don't cross that line everyone will die."

It was a besieged village. The epidemic had already killed about a third of the villagers and sickened maybe another third. What was this disease, and how was it transmitted? How did it start, and what determined who got ill and who did not, who died and who survived? I could not answer these questions without extensive testing, but there were things that I could do in the interim.

"We have to separate," I told the man who seemed to be the village chief.

"Separate?"

"Yes, separate the infected from everyone else to stop transmission, then we have to track – track the disease to its source. And we need to get help quickly."

"We'll do whatever you say," he told me.

He had asked me who I was, and I had told him the circumstances that brought me to the village.

"You came through the forest?" he asked in disbelief.

"Yes, I did. There was no other way."

"And you're not a spirit?"

Quarantining the sick was easier than tracking the disease and finding its patient zero. But the more villagers I spoke to as I charted a timeline, the more it appeared that the two-year-old son of the village chief was the first to be infected and to die. His father had returned from a trip with monkey meat, and his son had died three days after the family ate the meat. His wife died soon afterward. The village chief had fallen ill, but he had recovered. He was a trapper, and he had trapped the meat near a tributary that the villagers called White River. Why had the village chief not died? I wondered. Why had he recovered, and what did that say about the pathology of the disease?

The situation in the village was dire. Fortunately, I had brought some drugs and other supplies to manage symptoms. But my emergency kit provided at best only a temporary relief. I had to go back through the forest to get help.

"There's another way," the chief told me. "It's longer, but you ⊠ don't have to go back through the forest."

"I prefer the forest. Besides, we don't have much time."

And that was how we eventually stopped what became known as the White River Virus in a small village in the Congo before it could come through the forest.

When I awoke, I wasn't sure if I had been dreaming or remembering, if I was my grandfather or he was himself. It felt as if I had been doing both, as if I had been both. There was a vividness to it all that did not seem dream-like, but there were also forms that did not seem real. I had called Ivan back, and he had told me some of the stories that my grandfather had told him.

"Why did he tell you so much about the past if he was a man who had already left the past behind?" I asked him. "His former maid said he sometimes referred to his past as a previous lifetime."

"Maybe so, but this was different. Aileek – forgive me for still calling him that; it's burned into my brain – shared information he had that could help others save lives. Maybe that's why he spoke about his former missions. He was a missionary."

"Missionary?"

"I don't mean that in a religious sense. Our mission is to save lives. Period."

I almost envied Ivan his ability to end a sentence with "Period," as if there was nothing else to be said about it, no other truth. I tended to "overthink everything," as Ella would say. Joel would also sometimes ask me to "cool it." Sal would side with me. "Don't mind them. We need more sense in this world. Too many brains full of mush, that's the problem with the world." "Why do it with more when you can do it with less?" Ella would respond enigmatically. I missed them all.

I missed Ella very much. It had only been ten days since we parted, but it felt as if it had been longer than that – much longer. How would I be able to live in Memphis for a whole year, even if I went back and forth to Houston, without her? I had been asking myself that question for some time.

"Why don't you make video calls?" Nathan suggested when I told him how much I missed Ella even though we spoke on the phone every day."

"I don't like video calls. It makes me miss her more, not less."

"Really?"

"Yes, and she's like me that way."

I had been in Stellenbosch for ten days. I had only ten days before I had to resume teaching. In the time I had spent in South

Africa, I had learned so much about my grandfather that I could sometimes virtually see him sitting in a chair and studying his "wall of everything." It was as if the house itself, especially that long wall, was speaking to me. I could think and talk about him in a way that I never did before.

There were gaps in the stories about him that I would like to fill, and I considered making a stopover in London on my way back to Houston and Memphis. I would love to learn more about Ann Pottinger. But why her? There were pictures of other people on that wall that I didn't know or recognize. Who were they? How could I possibly track down or learn about everyone that my grandfather met or knew, if he actually met or knew these people? I couldn't, I told myself, but there was something about Ann Pottinger that felt different. Besides my grandmother, she was the only other person that my grandfather had scribbled a note beneath her image – about how much she loved sunsets. What did it mean? Was he referring to the supernal sunset in the picture or something else? What could that "something else" be?

Besides that note, my obsession – was that the right word? – with Ann Pottinger had to do with Uncle Ibe's story. But then he had been quite young at the time. Had he made up that story? I didn't believe so. My uncle was not that sort of person at all; he was a truth-teller. Even though the ogba ngbada brotherhood had been overshadowed by the crisscross of "modernity" discernible in my village, Uncle Ibe was still – and probably would always be – an ogba ngbada. To him, ogba ngbada was a sacrament of brotherhood and truth. "People think ogba ngbada is only about enchanting drums and forest spirits. It is to be as true to people as we are to the earth itself. And in the old days truth to the earth was non-negotiable, you already know that. The best hunters are kings of the forest, but what are forests but the hairs of the earth?" I had never known Uncle Ibe to tell a lie or even stretch the truth. Had he misremembered then? Time sometimes plays tricks with our memories. Perhaps, but everything else he told me was true. Why would this be different?

Maybe I was asking the wrong question, I considered. What if my grandfather had met Ann Pottinger in Nigeria, maybe in Fegge, instead of London? It was not uncommon for British citizens to vacation in Nigeria or simply visit in those days. Where was the picture actually taken? The glowing sunset had blinded possible indicators. Had that been deliberate? Had my grandfather in fact collected that picture because of the sunset? But that note in his handwriting suggested otherwise. I went back to the wall and studied that picture for the umpteenth time, but it had already yielded to me all the meaning that it was capable of. I had pondered the zenith of its sun; I was beginning to contemplate its sunset as if it were sunrise.

But I discovered something else. On a corner that I had not paid as much attention to as I should, there were ideograms that I recognized. A long time ago, people in and around my village used ideograms to hide or to reveal their secrets. I had studied some of these writing systems, and I recognized the ideograms as nsibidi. There were two signs that were repeated. The first was a commentary about the past, "Azubuike," and the other was a vision of the future, "Nkiruka." Where had my grandfather collected these signs or learned to write them? And he wasn't just writing them; he had created a pattern with them. At the base of that pattern was a lizard and a chameleon.

"One of the stories that Father told us," Uncle Ibe had recounted, "was about how the Creator sent the lizard and the chameleon from the sky with two different messages for everyone on earth. Whichever message was heard first would become the will of the Creator. The lizard was to announce human mortality – that everyone on earth would someday die. The chameleon was to proclaim human immortality – that everyone on earth would live forever. The lizard and the chameleon raced to earth on their different missions. But the chameleon was particular about the terrain, which is why our people named it 'Ogwumagana: If it sinks,

I won't pass.' The earth was still mushy because it was new and not fully formed, and the chameleon was concerned about finding the right path so that it would only tread on firm earth. As a result, it arrived at the square to make its proclamation after the lizard had already announced human mortality as the unalterable law of the Creator."

The past. The future. The lizard. The chameleon. What did all these mean? Did they even mean something together? My grandfather was a medical doctor when he left Fegge; he arrived Stellenbosch an artist. Was all this only visual poetry in a state of flux? Did everything on the wall have a separate meaning or was a cumulative meaning supposed to emerge from the interaction of all the elements? Were some of these meant to be an art of memory or were they all supposed to say something profound? My grandfather didn't seem to care about immortality; he did what he felt called upon to do. And he apparently created his own past and future, as if he was beyond time. Maybe he was just playing around with ideas and forms, which could be why he described the wall as a work in progress. Maybe I was overthinking again.

I called Ella.

"Slow down, Ile," she said after she had listened to my outpouring of words and thoughts. "You're confusing me. Your grandfather – King Lazarus, Ojadili, notOjadili, Monk – is now a lizard and a chameleon, the past and the future?"

"Did you even hear anything I said?"

"You were talking like a hurricane. Slow down."

I explained the new discoveries I had made on the wall.

"Come home, Ile," she said simply. "You can bring the wall back, I mean everything on the wall. Just come home."

"Why are you sounding like that?"

"Because this thing is beginning to do things to your mind, and every step in one direction leads to four new directions. Your grandfather was gone for forty-four years. That's a lifetime, and he was also a nomad. You can't possibly account for all that time."

"You're right, but I've learned so much from coming here."

"I'm glad. You had to go, but now it's time to come home."

"Look at you! Why don't you just say you're missing me instead of waxing philosophical about one road becoming ten other roads?"

She laughed. "Of course, I miss you, my No. 44."

It was a reminder that always made us laugh together.

"As for the road image, you said it better than I did," she added.

When I spoke with Joel, however, he thought I should consider going to London.

"Really? I thought you'd ask me to wrap it up."

"The London angle seems important. It's one thing not to get started, but once you do it's good to follow the leads as far as you can. Otherwise, you'll always wonder if you should or shouldn't have."

"That's true. But maybe the whole point of the gap is that there'll always be gaps anyway, unless I devote a lot more time or a lifetime to this."

"It's worth it, I think."

"Maybe I'll go to London. The problem is that I don't know where to go when I get there, and there's the possibility that this woman doesn't live in London at all."

"If you're not certain that she lives in London, then why were you talking about going there?"

I told him about Uncle Ibe.

"Your uncle was nine years old at the time? Well, I don't know any more."

"I'll figure it out."

"It seems you're finally on a cruise, only you don't know it yet."

"Me, a cruise? You wish."

We both laughed.

"How's Sal?"

"Beautiful, as always. The list of dishes that she plans to cook for your reception keeps getting longer."

"Reception?"

"To welcome you back. Just the four of us and a few other people."

When I put down the phone, I told myself that London could wait. With Ella asking me to come home, I decided that I would surprise her. I must be incredibly lucky, otherwise what did I do to deserve someone like her? I'll show her just how much she means to me. I'll return home early. I'll call ahead to that restaurant in Galveston Bay that she loves so much, and I'll take her there that night. We often went to seafood restaurants to celebrate something special. But seafood was also where our culinary tastes diverged. Ella loved everything from the sea – especially lobsters and prawns – and I could barely stand to look at them. There was something in my brain that expected these lobsters and prawns to suddenly come to life either on the dinner table or in the stomach.

"Why are you paranoid about seafood?" Ella always wondered.

"Maybe because I think the stomach has a lot of fluids," I sometimes responded mischievously.

"So, you think they'll wake up, even after digestion, and start swimming?"

"Or maybe because they don't look dead in the first place. When you're served a steak, it doesn't look like a cow. But these things look as if they're only slumbering in some sort of maritime sun."

"Ile!"

"Don't mind me. Enjoy."

"I will. You don't know what you're missing."

Whatever it was, I was happy to be missing it. But I liked the ambience of seafood restaurants, that feeling that everyone exuded – both the patrons and the waiters – that this wasn't just any other restaurant; this was a seafood paradise, nothing less. I liked the way that people ate their prawns and lobsters, even shrimps and crawfish, as if they were dining on food for the gods. It wasn't like a burger shop where people ate something sticky between hamburger buns, something that dribbled down the side of their mouths as if they were truck drivers making a quick stop after they had lost their way on the interstate. "Seafood" meant "extra special," and I liked that. Ella always insisted that the seafood restaurants around Galveston Bay were the best anywhere.

I didn't have too much left to do in South Africa, so it was easy to wind up quickly. I had already signed the necessary legal papers. There was one more thing I had to do, something I had kept until the very last. I went with Willem to the cemetery to pay my respects to my grandfather. My head kept telling me that I shouldn't forgive him for leaving his family the way he did. But in my heart I still loved him. In the end, I told myself that maybe some things are so complicated, so nuanced, that they're beyond the usual choices. My grandfather was untranslatable in that sense.

I didn't like cemeteries. In my village, we buried people in the same compound they had lived in all their lives. Both the dead and the living shared a common space. My grandfather had been "buried" in his compound; his gravesite proclaimed his name and his birthdate as well as death date. Aunt Rosette had added a sign of the cross; my father had had King Lazarus carved on the gravestone; and Uncle Ibe had carved a symbol that he said was the mark of the truest ogba ngbada. In Stellenbosch, my grandfather's tombstone was different. It only contained two words: "The Monk." There was no date of birth, no date of death. That tombstone was at once eloquent and taciturn at the same time, but perhaps that was to be expected.

As I stood there, so many thoughts swirled inside my head.

If I could actually see my grandfather, what would I say to him? He had been such a presence all my life even though I never met him. Hearing about him, thinking about him, trailing him had taught me lessons – intended or unintended – that I hoped I would always remember. What could I say to him? I kneeled down, cupped my hands, whispered into them, then I opened my hands to the two-word testament that proclaimed: "The Monk."

    It was in that cemetery that the idea came to me about what to do with the house. I had been wondering about that. I didn't plan to move to Stellenbosch and I wasn't looking to own a summer home, so I knew I wouldn't live there although I would have liked to. Willem had advised me to sell. It was prime property in the very best neighborhood, he said. "Oh, they'll snap it up in a second and you'll make loads of money." My father had left his wealth, and much of it was my grandfather's, to me. And then my grandfather had also left his recent wealth to me. I wasn't looking for more money, and I wasn't keen on the idea of selling the house. My grandfather had returned from the dead forty-four years, four months, and four days after his death, and he had lived in that house. And that meant something inexpressible to me. I would take everything on the wall. But the house?

    "I've made a decision about the house," I told Willem as we left the cemetery.

    "Good. Should I call the agent? Actually, I can give you her number. She'll take care of everything. I'll do the rest, including getting the money to you."

    "I'm not selling the house. I've decided to give it away."

    "Why would you do something like that?"

    He took a look at my face and decided not to press the point. "What charity do you want to give it to?" he inquired instead.

    "No, I'll give it to Thelma."

    "Why?" he asked in his measured voice.

    "I know her story. She's one person, but she's also a clan.

There are many people counting on her. Besides, my grandfather was an old man. Someone had to take care of him at that age, and she did."

"She was well paid."

"She took care of him in a way that was priceless."

"Why didn't your grandfather bequeath the house to her?"

"Because he gave it to me. He knew I'd know what to do. He didn't know me, but he knew me. And he trusted me. My grandfather was King Lazarus in his other life. He raised the dead. This is what he would have done under these circumstances."

Willem shook his head as if my decision was beyond him. Or maybe he wasn't really surprised. After all, he knew and worked for my grandfather.

When I told Thelma I was giving her the house, she broke down and cried. I thought they were only tears of joy, but she soon began to sing the same song she said she had sung for my grandfather, began slowly as if she was seeing something approaching from a distant horizon, then her voice quivered up an incline as if she wanted to see even better what was arriving or returning. It was a farewell lament, but it was also a song of reunion. There was something heart-rending about it all, as if seeing my grandfather in me brought Thelma grievous sadness as well as uplifting joy.

"I can't thank you enough," she told me, wiping her tears, "but you know I can't live in that house. A mansion in Stellenbosch, in the elite neighborhood in Stellenbosch – for me? Ha! Maybe in another lifetime."

Thelma had spent all her life in townships, and that had done something to her that I wasn't sure she wholly realized. In another lifetime, she said, her life would be different.

"I grew up in Khayelitsha," she reminded me. "I have many fond childhood memories, don't misunderstand me, but Khayelitsha is that part of Cape Town that slaughters the spirit."

I must have seen a different part of the city, I thought – its proud horns, not its rump.

"That's why I'm giving you the house," I told her. "My grandfather only gave you the door as a promise. I'm giving you the house in fulfillment of that promise. You can live in it with your family. I hope you do. Or Willem can help you sell it or rent it out if that's what you prefer. I've already signed the transfer documents and spoken to him. It will be well, Thelma – and in this lifetime."

"Enkosi, enkosi. uThixo akysikelele."

I spent two more days in Stellenbosch. It was enough time to take down the artifacts on the wall and entrust them to Willem to freight to me as soon as possible. Thelma sang the train song for me on the day of my departure. "I pray that I'll see you again in this lifetime," she told me. "It was God that brought your grandfather here." That song, and the way she sang it, was a powerful reminder of the funereal songs that Kayamandi had sung for my grandfather. Those songs, those freedom songs that they had deemed fit to honor my grandfather with as if his coming went farther back in time than they initially thought, and that wall in my grandfather's living room – they will always haunt me.

The Book of Everything

4

I stopped over in Lagos on my way back to Houston. I had planned to visit Abuja, but I wanted to get home earlier. I had surprised Ella once with an early return, and she had danced around the apartment as if I had dropped from the moon. And I had been gone for only three days to a four-day conference. This should be something special.

As soon as I settled down in my hotel room, I called Aunt Rosette and Uncle Ibe. Nathan had picked me up from the airport, but he had left to run an errand for his mother-in-law, who was presently visiting them. He would be back to take me to dinner in his house.

"How are you, Ile?" my aunt asked. "You're calling me with a Nigerian number, so I assume you're in Nigeria."

"Yes, I'm in Lagos. I'm leaving for Houston tomorrow, so I won't be able to visit Abuja as promised."

"Ah, Ile! I was looking forward to seeing you."

"Same here, auntie, but I need to go."

"What's the rush? Surely, you can spend a few more days in Nigeria."

"I've got quite a bit to do before I resume teaching."

"Hmm, Ile, are you sure that's why you're rushing back?"

"What else could it be?"

"You know, and I know, what else it could be," she said with a chuckle. I could almost see her winking. My aunt could be naughty sometimes. "Well, you two should hurry up; we need more babies in the family."

"We'll get there, auntie."

"You're already there, in Jesus name."

I said an "Amen." Aunt Rosette was a "modern Christian," which meant whatever she wanted it to mean at any time, but she liked to hear an "Amen" whenever she said a prayer or invoked the name of God.

"How was your trip to South Africa?" she asked me, a bit

tentatively, as if she wanted to know but also did not want to know. "Did you find out anything?" Her tone had become challenging.

Until then, I had not quite decided how to respond to that question, which I knew she – and my uncle – would eventually ask.

"No, auntie. It was a mix-up. My grandfather was King Lazarus; this man was Monk."

"I told you so," she said triumphantly, as if one person could not be King Lazarus and Monk. "Are you satisfied now, you doubting Thomas?"

"I am."

It was best, I told myself, to let my aunt go on believing what she chose or what agreed with her spirit.

Uncle Ibe was different. There was no challenge in his voice, only curiosity.

"What did you find out about your grandfather?" he asked me.

"Oh, it was a mix-up," I told him. "They confused someone called Monk with King Lazarus.

"Monk. King Lazarus," he said slowly, as if probing the words for illumination. "Aren't they the same thing?"

"How so?"

"Someone who's King Lazarus probably has to be a monk."

"Maybe, but not the other way round," I said, surprised at the turn the conversation was taking.

"You think so? Anyway, you found Monk, not King Lazarus. But you didn't answer my question."

"I did, uncle. It was a mix-up. You were right about my grandfather."

"Right about what?"

"He died a long time ago."

"No matter how old a lion gets, Ile, it does not eat grass."

I didn't know whether he was agreeing or disagreeing with me, and there was no point asking him to interpret his proverb. My uncle never did that. "A proverb is like half a word," he would say. "If it gets into the right mind, it becomes whole." I would complain that he was explaining one proverb with another one, and he would smile and say "It's the way the world was given to us." Sometimes, my uncle sounded like an ancient mariner beached on an island and bravely translating his sorrow into joy. He would probably have been happier in what he called "the old world" but he seemed to have made his peace with the present.

"I don't understand, uncle," I said anyway. "Who's the lion and what's the grass?"

"You don't know? No matter how long a macaw flies, it will never turn into an eagle."

My uncle had such a youngish spirit that I sometimes spoke to him familiarly as if we were age-mates.

"Is this what you do in your restaurant these days – sit back and dream up proverbs?" I asked him.

He laughed so loud and long that I began to chuckle myself.

"You'll kill me one day, Ile. You say such funny things. As for the restaurant, you refused to come to Abuja so that we can feed you properly. Maybe one day I'll come to America and open a restaurant so that I can feed all of you there properly. When you feed the stomach properly, the brain rejoices."

"You, come to America? That will be the day. I'll buy you a first-class ticket."

"Why not put me in the cockpit?" he said with a laugh. "But it'll probably happen one day. Haven't you noticed that in this world everything eventually happens? Just give it time."

I had said the same thing, in a different context, to Willem just a few days ago.

"Seriously, it would have been nice to see you again. I

know we saw each other not so long ago, but the older you get the more important presence becomes. You do remember that you promised to finally return home soon?"

"I remember, uncle."

"As for Father, I don't know what happened in South Africa or what's going on in your mind right now, but I know that one day you'll tell me the truth."

"I already did, uncle. It was a mix-up, believe me."

"So be it then," he said with something that sounded like a sigh.

I had thought of asking Uncle Ibe a few more questions about Ann Pottinger, but I reconsidered. I wondered: Did my uncle somehow believe or suspect that my grandfather had not died in 1974 or was he simply hoping for some sort of resurrection? Whatever it was, he did sound rather relieved when I insisted that my trip to South Africa only confirmed that my grandfather died when they thought he did. I had provided the confirmation they seemed to still need. But...why had I done that? It was what my grandfather would have wanted, I told myself. But was it?

Later that night, after Agatha had graciously overfed us, I went out with Nathan so we could talk "like boys" over a few more drinks.

"How was your trip?" Nathan asked me. "You didn't give details over the phone."

"What I'm about to tell you, Nathan, you must promise never ever to tell anybody else, including your wife."

He looked at me as if I had become unhinged. "What's the matter with you, Ile? Has living in America done things to your brain?"

Nathan and I had protected each other's secrets like gold nuggets since I could remember. Sometimes, both of us would be punished because neither of us would reveal who had committed an offense. "It must be one of you," Nathan's father would say through clenched teeth. "If you don't tell me who, I won't give the offender six lashes; I'll give both of you twelve lashes each." That was back in the days when parents could discipline their children's friends without being tarred and feathered for doing so. We both knew that Nathan's father, a man who earned his living with his muscles, could give painful lashes that maddened the skin. Twelve lashes from him was like a death sentence, but we kept quiet nevertheless and braced for the slaying.

"Forgive me," I said, "but I don't want this to get back to my uncle and auntie. I found my grandfather in South Africa."

"You did what?"

"I mean, I found that he lived there until recently. That attorney was right. He only died about four months ago."

I told him everything.

"Unbelievable! How are you dealing with this?" he asked me.

"What do you mean?"

"It sort of blows the mind. I was almost certain that you'd come back with a different kind of news. How do you handle something like this?"

"I wouldn't have known how, but I think that maybe that was why he created that wall, or at least one of the reasons. That wall spoke to me. It told me things that could not be expressed in any language."

"That wall...spoke to you? What are you talking about?"

"I'm serious. I now know or understand things that I have no language to explain. Language is still evolving, my friend, but it hasn't caught up – and probably will never catch up – with the flux of emotions. Haven't you ever felt that way?"

"What way?"

"Sometimes, something happens to you or you feel something and you grapple with the right words to say it. But there's no right word, no word so nuanced or spectral that it suffices, but you settle for a word anyway. The language of emotion is not always the language of expression. Maybe that's why we need poetry, a certain kind of poetry. Still, some things are untranslatable. If I hadn't gone to South Africa, I'm not sure I would have known how to deal with this."

"I think I understand what you're saying," Nathan said slowly. "Sometimes, we're lost for words..."

"That's close, but I'm talking about something different. Think about looking at a great painting or listening to great music and then having to put in words what you feel about its aura. This is even deeper than that. There are simply no words in any language to express it. When I went to the cemetery to pay my respects to my grandfather, I kneeled before his grave and whispered 'I understand.'"

"You do?"

"Yes. Not everything but enough."

"What do you understand?"

"You're being lawyerly and not listening to me enough, Nathan. I don't have the words to explain it."

Nathan laughed. He was used to me taking jabs at his "lawyerly instincts." "But you're a professor of English," he said. "You've mastered all the words."

"Indeed. What am I – the Encyclopedia Britannica? I do know that our dictionaries keep getting bigger. We've gone from a single volume to multiple volumes, but it's an impossible project – to create a vocabulary of consciousness that matches words to every possible nuance of feeling."

"You're going deeper into the forest, Ile."

Our people sometimes said that – "going deeper into the forest" – when someone began to leave behind the familiar terrain of experience and expression.

"That's where my grandfather took me – deeper and deeper into the forest until it seemed that I had become him."

"You became your grandfather?"

"I had this dream that wasn't a dream, and in that experience it seemed that we were one."

"But that's how dreams go. Anything can happen in them."

"I know. This is not the first dream that I've ever had. But, I tell you, this was different."

"You know what I think, Ile? You need to go home, to someone real, and clear your head."

"I'm on my way, but that doesn't change anything I've told you."

I did not really expect Nathan, or anyone else, to understand something that I was still grappling with in an unmapped region of my mind.

BANDA ACEH – Ten years after a tsunami struck the city of Banda Aceh on Dec. 26, 2004, killing 167,000 people, roads and bridges have been rebuilt, there are houses on the beach, trees have grown back and the millions of tons of debris that covered the island are gone. But reminders of the disaster seem to be everywhere.

A sculpture of a giant wave marks Lambaro, one of four mass grave sites, where 46,000 bodies are buried. A hotel front desk displays a photo of smashed boats filling its parking lot. The dome from a mosque 1½ km away rests in an emerald-green rice field.

Water streams down the cavelike walls of the Tsunami Museum, which serves as both a memorial and evacuation site, with a knoll on high ground offering refuge in case another tsunami strikes. The center of the museum is an atrium that rises above a park, decorated with the word "Peace" and the flags of countries that provided assistance. Exhibits explain how the community worked together to rebuild, and how the formerly embattled province even found ways to make peace after the disaster, with rebels in a long and bloody separatist fight signing a deal with the central government.

Only three natural disasters in the last century have killed more people: More than 1 million people died in flooding in China in 1931; a cyclone left more than 300,000 dead in Bangladesh in 1970; and an earthquake in China killed at least 255,000 people in 1976.

Almost everyone in Banda Aceh has a story to share.
– The Japan Times, *December 21, 2014*

    I arrived in Houston two days after leaving Stellenbosch. Everything felt a bit different – like something lost and later found or something forgotten and rediscovered. I knew what everything was, but I apparently needed a bit of time to get used to the things I already knew. Fortunately, I ran into Osita, and I knew I was certainly back in Houston Nigeriana.

    Osita was what Ella would describe as a "real person." I did not usually participate in the thousand and one events hosted by different people in the Nigerian community, especially during the summer, but I've been to a few of them. Osita seemed to attend them all, because I saw him everywhere I went. I noticed him because he was always well-dressed without being flamboyant. I thought his overall style – his sense of color and texture and pattern – was impeccable, and I concluded that he probably worked in the fashion industry. Was he a designer or a marketer? Once, I heard the sort of floating talk common at such events that he worked at the airport and I assumed that, well, he must be a manager or a technical expert. Or was he a pilot?

    All my assumptions evaporated the day I sat next to Osita and we fell into conversation. He said he had seen me before and that I carried myself well. I thanked him for the compliment. I was used to people not revealing their occupations at these events – except perhaps for medical doctors, pharmacists, engineers, registered nurses, and professors. Osita told me his name but added that he often asked white people to simply call him "O" or "Oz" because he didn't like the way they often mispronounced his name.

"I work at the airport, airport security," he told me.

I was surprised. "You're a policeman?" I asked.

"No, airport security. Me, policeman? That would be something."

I introduced myself, and Osita did most of the talking after that – as if he had been looking forward to talking to me for a long time. He wasn't one of those people who was still dreaming of returning to Nigeria, he said. He had accepted that he would die and be buried in America.

"I already left Nigeria. I don't want to spend the rest of my life crying about it. I tell you, I'm no longer an immigrant. How can you still be an immigrant after you've lived in a country for twenty-five years? That's one generation. After one generation, even half a generation, you're either in or out. I'm here to stay, and I've been here for almost thirty years."

I was a bit surprised by the clarity of his thoughts. I didn't know if I agreed with him or not, but he gave the impression that he had thought about his situation carefully.

"It looks like you've done a lot of thinking about these things," I said.

"I certainly have. I was a truck driver for a long time. The interstate can be a very lonely place with only the road and the wind for company, and it can make you think about your whole life three or five or even ten times over. You think about things that are best forgotten until you almost begin to go crazy. Some drivers said it was sleep that troubled them on these long hauls. For me, it was my mind. It troubled me so much that I gave up the job. It was a good job, and I made more money then than I do now. But I had to give it up. I'm busier at the airport, and there's often a crowd passing through, so I don't have the time to replay and regret my whole life."

Osita had come to America right after high school. He had been admitted to study Biomedical Engineering at Johns Hopkins University.

"Johns Hopkins, Biomedical Engineering?"

"No less. I wasn't a bad student. I now wish I had stayed focused and finished my degree, but I had more youth than sense in those days. I thought the true America was the one I saw in the movies. I partied as if the clubs were going into extinction, and I chased women as if they had just been created. I did too much of everything that I probably shouldn't have done, and then I ran into trouble in my second year. I was in the wrong place at the wrong time, and I was arrested for doing drugs. I tell you, I've never done drugs in my life. But I could have been trying to wake up a frozen sea with hymns. No one believed me. I went to jail for something that I never did, and that was how my studentship ended. Our people sometimes say it's better to go to prison in America than in Nigeria because American prisons are better. I tell you, a prison is a no-good place, even a prison in paradise. I was facing possible deportation, but then I met a prison counselor and we got along so well that she married me."

The marriage came to a nasty end after Osita was released. Osita had met his wife in the prison clinic where he went because he wasn't feeling well. She was a registered nurse and a fellow Nigerian. They got talking, and she took an interest in him. But Osita thought right away that she was too good for him. How could he, a scoundrel, be deserving of such a polished woman? So, he did nothing to pursue the relationship, even though he wanted to. She did. And that was how it came about that she married him, as he phrased it – "out of respect for her courage and forthrightness." She waited for him and tried to help rehabilitate him after he came out of prison. But Osita kept thinking that he was too undeserving to be receiving such attention. He began to suspect that she must have an ulterior motive, otherwise how could she be in love with him? "You can go from one corner of Texas to the other, you'll never find a bigger fool than the one speaking to you right now," he said in that self-deprecating manner that he had. "Everything was going well, but instead of feeling blessed I thought it was too good to be true. And I ruined it all like a royal idiot."

He wouldn't tell me how he "ruined it all like a royal idiot," but whatever it was brought the marriage to a nasty end. Osita was once more free to bemoan his fate, the same one that he was foisting on himself.

"I tell you, I have a talent for messing things up," he said. "I was the kind of person that you would throw a rope to save his life and he would first of all question your motives or sniff at your kindness as if it was a ploy to lead him unsuspectingly to his doom. But that was then. I'm not one of those who run around crying that I spent some of the best years of my life in prison. I did, sadly. I was there for ten years for something I didn't do, but I was thirty when I came out. I could have started all over, but I didn't. I don't know what it was but something seemed to have gone wrong with my mind. I felt indelibly stained in a way that I couldn't explain, so I continued fighting my conviction. Fortunately, my attorney, a white American woman, was a dynamo. My conviction was eventually overturned, and I received a large compensation. Suddenly, it was as if I hadn't learned anything. I began partying all over again. I tell you, money is a spirit. There's nothing else to explain what happened to me. I went wild as if there was no tomorrow.

"One of the earliest songs that I fell in love with was by Fleetwood Mac: 'Don't stop thinking about tomorrow, don't stop, it'll soon be here.' After I got my compensation, I wondered what the hell they were singing about. I soon learned. The day I wrote a check and it bounced back to me I couldn't believe it. I was sure

I had a lot more money in the bank. Well, I consoled myself, I had a good run. But I had forgotten to die. I was still alive, which meant I had to figure out a way to earn a living. Someone told me truck-driving was it, so I trained to become a truck driver. I made so many bad choices that I've crowned myself the King of Idiots. I don't blame anyone, but my life is such a mess I don't even know what to do."

I wouldn't have known how to respond to his story, but he had been so open that it wasn't difficult for me to say: "You can start all over again. In fact, you should. You can still go to Johns Hopkins and study Biomedical Engineering if you want to. If you could do it the first time, there's no reason why you can't do it again. I suggest you call the school, then do what you have to."

"I'm nearing fifty," he told me like someone announcing that he had been diagnosed with a terminal disease.

"That's the perfect age to start over," I said as if I knew what I was talking about.

He looked at me thoughtfully. "Are you Nigerian?" he asked.

"One hundred percent."

"You don't really talk like one. And it's not what you say. People have told me the same thing before. It's the way you say it."

"How?"

"I can't describe it. You say it as if it's the most natural thing in the world, no pain. In this country, you can start over at any age. It's OK. But in Nigeria, some people begin to project your death date when you turn fifty. The government begins to fast-track your retirement and people treat you as if you've become an antediluvian reptile sunning its scales for the last time. That's why I've decided I can't live in that country again. Plus other reasons."

"No, we respect old age in Nigeria; we don't revile it."

"I tell you, sometimes the difference is kind of blurry. If

you eat in a certain way people ask you 'Are you a child?' If you dance in a certain fashion they ask you 'Are you a baby?' If you want to start over, they tell you 'Your time has passed. Haba!'"

"But it only matters if you listen."

"It's not just what they say; there are other signals."

"I don't think ageism has anything to do with being Nigerian. It's the world."

"Maybe."

"I'll help you," I promised, "in any way that I can."

Osita was older than me, but it seemed to me that what he needed was a mentor, the right kind of mentor.

"God will bless you," he said. "You're a young man, and you're Nigerian. I tell you, I was wrong. I take back everything I said."

"It's a big country. It's so big that there's a lot of diversity within. It's like Houston. Too many Nigerian parties, right? But there are lots of Nigerians here who are powering this country with their brains. The world is always bigger than our little corner. All we have to do is look over our picket fence."

"That's why you're a professor, and you talk like one."

We laughed.

"I feel like I've already been to the future," he said. "I mean, twenty or thirty years ago, whenever I thought about the future it was about where I would be in ten or twenty or thirty years' time. I'm there now, and I'm so disappointed with myself that I want to crawl into a corner and die. You can't even imagine the sort of dreams that I had in those days."

"So, start over."

"I don't know. I've also met some people who've accomplished so much in their lives but either look back with a tinge of regret because they had expected to achieve even more or seem to realize that in the end virtually everything is pointless. One of them told me that when he was young he used to think that God was a tragedian, which was why the Son of God died on the cross to save the world. Thirty years later, he's not sure what to think. In my own case, I demonstrated enough idiocy to ruin an entire village."

"You're not an idiot. Everyone makes mistakes. You'll only be an idiot if you don't start over."

I didn't see Osita after that. Our conversation had been seriously interrupted, after several minor interruptions, and we had forgotten to exchange addresses.

"I've been looking for you," he told me when I ran into him at the airport. "Someone said you've returned to Nigeria. You see how people spread false information? I can't thank you enough, my brother. You saved my life. There was something about the way you spoke to me that lifted a huge cloud and pushed me to do what I needed to."

He had applied – and been admitted again – to study Biomedical Engineering at Johns Hopkins.

"You can see I'm not wearing a uniform," he said as if I had ever seen him in a uniform. "I resigned from airport security. I'm on my way back to Baltimore – Johns Hopkins. They gave me a scholarship too. It's like you brought me back from the dead."

I'd never been happier. Well, I've probably been. Still, I'd never been happier. I wished Osita well, and we exchanged addresses properly this time.

"I'll throw a party for you whenever you're back in Houston, a big one," I told him.

Meeting Osita put me in an even more buoyant mood for what I was sure would be a stirring reunion with Ella. I couldn't wait to get home. I called a limousine to take me home, then to wait for Ella to get ready for our ride to Galveston Bay. This time, I would try to do more than just admire the prawns and lobsters. It would be a night like no other.

And it was. But not in the way I had fantasized. I walked

in on a naked Ella and Joel writhing and moaning in our bed. Ella was on top, something that she did only when she was quite excited, and her bulbous butt was going up and down as if it was possessed. In the background was a hip-hop song that proclaimed the persona of the artist "the greatest, from Pharaoh to Playboy," the sort of music that she especially liked when she felt "wild, like the wilderness" – whatever that meant. Usually, she played jazz more than any other type of music. "You and I, we're the perfect jazz song," she would say. Not anymore obviously, if ever. They had locked the front door but had not bothered to close the bedroom door. They must have seen or sensed me, because Ella's frenzy ceased. She screamed, jumped up, and bounded away to a corner of the room with her hands in front of her as if she was warding off a special kind of evil. In her flight, she knocked over the CD player that she had positioned close to the bed and the music stopped in the middle of a phallic boast. She didn't try to explain anything to me or to claim that what I saw was not what I thought it was, as if she already considered any such explanation unlikely to appease the demon of anger within me. Instead, she began to whimper a frenzy of words and phrases – "Holy Michael," "Mother Mary," "Blessed Heart," "Divine Mercy" – as if she was exorcising an evil that threatened her very existence.

My mind told me that everything I was looking at was impossible, unreal, but how could that be when I was looking at them? A long time ago, I had been accosted by armed robbers in Fegge. The leader of the gang began to walk toward me with his gun held out as if he was about to shoot. I knew my life was about to end, but what I saw in front of me were mostly dancing masquerades. Fortunately, one of the robbers identified me as the grandson of King Lazarus. The leader apologized to me and let me go. Was that what was happening to me now? But it couldn't be. I wasn't seeing masquerades or anything of that sort. I was looking at a naked Joel speaking gibberish as he tried to say something to me and also cover his nakedness – in my matrimonial bed. I was looking at a naked Ella whimpering and warding off whatever, the same Ella, my wife, that I had seen writhing with ecstasy on top of my best friend some seconds ago. Why didn't she try and cover her nakedness too? I wondered. Or did she somehow think that her "fresh breasts with kissy nipples," as I usually described them, would save her?

There were so many questions that possessed my mind at once. How on God's earth could something like this happen – Ella cheating on me with Joel or even with anyone whatsoever? How did this make any sense? Joel had wanted to kill himself after his girlfriend cheated on him with his best friend then. Ella's sister had been murdered for cheating on her "former" husband. Joel was my best friend. Ella was the best friend to Joel's wife. Ella was a professor of music who knew about harmony and resonance. Joel was a TV personality and psychiatrist who knew about the trajectories of the mind. How on God's earth could something like this happen? How had it even started? When? Why? How was I so blind that I never noticed anything untoward between Ella and Joel? Did that glance the last time we were together mean more than I thought it did? Or the way their shoulders touched when Sal called for a group hug, was there a meaning to that that should have been obvious to me? Was I so much a fool that I was unaware of my own foolishness? Pastor Isaiah used to proclaim that "The devil finds work for idle minds." But Joel was married, so how idle could he be? And Ella knew I would be back in two days. Or had I, and perhaps Sal, become so insufferable? Then, why was she pressing me to return home soon? In those days, my uncle would retort: "I pity the devil. He gets a bad rap for all the evil things that we do to one another. The problem of the world is not the devil. It's greed." Was that what I was witnessing? Sal wasn't enough for Joel and I wasn't enough for Ella? But what about honor and trust and friendship and conscience and love? Of all the women in the world, why Ella, my wife? Of all the men in the world, why Joel, my best friend? There were more questions than my mind could process at the same time.

Until I walked through my bedroom door that night, they were among my favorite people in the world – Ella and Joel. Nathan had become my brother, so I considered Joel my best friend. But how much did I really know about him or Ella? How much was it possible for anyone to know anyone else? What did it even mean to know anyone – in being or in spirit? I found myself asking myself. When everything was seemingly going as it should, I had considered any contrary indicators unimportant. Now, they bobbed to the surface insistently, pointing to possibilities that I had previously dismissed as ungrounded. Joel always talked about his love for cruising, but in all the time that I had known him he had never gone on a single cruise. I sometimes wondered about that, but I always shrugged it off. After some time, his stories about cruises began to sound more or less the same, in a way that raised a few questions in my mind. It was as if he was telling the same story, with some modifications, over and over again.

"When you're on a cruise," I asked him, "do you see the water?"

He looked at me with a puzzled face. "What do you mean? The boat sails on water, doesn't it? It'd be insane for it to sail on land, wouldn't it?" he asked with that charming smile of his.

"I know," I said. "I was just wondering. "Don't mind me. It's nothing."

"Oh, come on, say it. It's clear there's something going on in that head of yours."

"Well, if you insist..."

"I do."

"I asked because your cruise stories are never about admiring or pondering or watching or anything to do with water, day or night. They're usually about the lodgings or the entertainment, those kinds of things – the room types, the view upward or downward from the bed, even the type of locks, the cuisine, the ballroom, the music, the dancing, you know."

He laughed. "But that's what a cruise is all about. You can gaze at the water in any hotel pool. People go on a cruise for the ultimate experience." He rolled the words "ultimate experience" as if he had just created the combination, the perfect phrase to express a concept so complex and interrelated that my non-cruising mind might not be able to grasp it. I wanted to point out that the water in a hotel pool could not be compared to the majesty of the sea and that I had heard other cruise tales with plenty of dining and dancing in them as well as the magic and mystery of the sea. I concluded instead that Joel's kind of cruise was different. After all, travelers on the same journey do not have the same experiences and insights simply because the route is the same. Besides, why stretch the point? But there was something pressing me to do so.

"There's this guy I met who crossed the Mediterranean Sea into Europe," I said. "He has horrible stories to tell about the wretched conditions on the crowded raft he was in, the immense peril of the journey, human greed, and the deviousness of the human mind. But, beyond all that or because of all that, he has incredible stories about the water itself that are etched on my mind. Sometimes, it's almost as if I was there. Maybe it's just the different ways that people tell stories."

"What kind of stories?" he asked me with a look of interest.

"There's the sound of the water. He said he never knew that water was so alive. And the sounds were not the same. Sometimes, it was a roll or a screech or a roar or a rumble and a range of other sounds that always meant something. So, he concluded that water speaks. It has a language, but perhaps we don't understand that language well enough yet. When he told the story, he went on and on from one type of sea sound to another in his imitation of the language of the waves."

"Interesting, very interesting," Joel said slowly.

I had expected a different kind of reaction. I thought he

would have something to say about his personal experience of the phenomenon instead of looking as if I was signaling to him the frontiers of a new world.

"This guy also spoke about the light—"

"In the water?"

"Yes, but it's not really a light in the same way you turn on the living room lights. It seemed he was talking about a different kind of light, but it came from the water."

"You mean a reflection?"

"No, he was talking about how there was a sort of light in the water at night, so it's probably not a reflection."

"And he could see this light?"

"I have the feeling that it was more like sensing the light. I still have some questions, more questions in fact than answers."

"Well, this guy was crossing the sea on a raft, you said. He was trying to steal into Europe. He had a different type of experience, an interesting one, but that's not cruising."

I was surprised by Joel's response. When I heard the story about the sound and the light in the water, I didn't know whether to believe it as a true account or to understand it as the sort of exaggeration that people who've been through traumatic experiences sometimes use – wittingly or unwittingly. I had hoped that Joel would draw from his own knowledge reservoir to confirm or question the story, but instead he was looking at me like a fresh-faced student sitting cross-legged before an ancient oracle. I did wonder then if someone could indeed go on so many cruises and love them as much as Joel did without knowing more about water or having personal stories other than the type of information that it was possible to gain by leafing through a catalog about cruises. Or did Joel perhaps have something else in mind when he talked about cruises. Had he been "cruising" with Ella? Was that why Ella chose him as our psychiatrist? I had never asked her how she chose Joel because I had concluded that she must have seen him on TV.

But Ella only watched TV when there was nothing else to do or while checking the channels before or after watching a movie. Had she stumbled on Joel's program? If she did, how did she know where his office was? I had considered such questions superfluous at the time. But were they?

Joel was born in Scarborough, England, a seaside resort where his father ran a small bed and breakfast. His earliest memories were related to the coastline and tourists. Many of the tourists who poured into Scarborough to experience "the original seaside resort" had all sorts of stories that made Joel connect the water to travel and travel to something so big that it was undefinable. He loved Scarborough, and this love was as much about the scenery and the seaside as it was about the town as some sort of wonderland that reeled in the world beyond. All that ended when his father passed away. His mother sold the bed and breakfast and moved to London. Joel felt like someone yanked away from the sea and marooned in an unfriendly territory. London was too cramped, too gloomy, too proper for his taste. He began to imagine a return back to a seaside wonderland, and it didn't have to be Scarborough. He had it all planned out, but his life took a different course. When he told me this story, it was easy to see that he felt he had somehow missed the boat he had longed for all through the "ugly" years in London – until he went on a cruise. He had won the first prize in a TV lottery, and the award was an all-expenses-paid Caribbean cruise. This first cruise was the only one that Joel ever described vividly as if it truly happened. It was also the only cruise story of his that included a reflection on the "awesomeness" of the sea. Was it possible that this singular cruise had become the sole source of his numerous cruise stories? But, even if it was, what did that mean other than that he was a daydreamer?

Ella was also a bit like that, sometimes embellishing actual events in ways that made them unrecognizable. The day I listened to her describe my "marriage proposal" to her on a boat in the middle of Galveston Bay, I briefly wondered if she had somehow mistaken me for Joel. That was the sort of thing that Joel would dream of doing, not someone like me who would only take a ride around Galveston Bay or any other sea inlet under extreme compulsion. Why did she even consider such a tale necessary? My proposal had been simple but it had also been thoughtful. I had chosen to treat her to a candle-lit dinner. I still remembered what she said that night when she walked into my apartment, No. 44: "You're supposed to be waiting for me with candle lights, the whole works." If she also thought my proposal was beautiful, as she sometimes said, why did she still feel the need to broadcast a fable instead?

As simple as it was, that candle-lit dinner had required thought and skill. When I went to a store that sold candles and all sorts of romantic items, my intention was simple – to buy some white candles. When I asked a store assistant to direct me to the right row, she pointed to a row that had more variety than I had even known existed. There were American candles, Egyptian, South African, Roman, Greek, Russian, and so many other nationalities of candles. It was almost as if the candles were canvases for so many artists who had disdained or been defeated by the conventional canvas. Each painting seemed more fantastical than the one before, each splash of color more experimental than the next. What was this – a riot of dots or a cross? Was this an image from a moonlight dance or from a bear hunt? And this – a lizard's tail or a gecko's jaw? I was confused. I eventually chose Egyptian candles for no other reason than that I heard another shopper say to someone on the phone that the Egyptian candles she bought the last time were scented, but she wasn't sure about the one she was presently looking at. I decided to take a chance. That was how I sometimes made store purchases, especially when I had no clear preference. I would go into a store to buy a simple item and then vacillate forever between several different kinds. If another shopper picked one type while I was looking and thinking,

I usually considered that a good sign if I liked the mien of the shopper. Ella always laughed at my "so-called method." She would ask me: "So, how did you decide this time? Was it a he or she, tall or short, white or black, American or not, cool or geeky?"

Besides the candles, I wanted to surprise Ella with a Nigerian meal that she had never eaten. But this was more difficult than it should be, I thought. Ella had gone deep into Houston Nigeriana, and she could recite a long list of Nigerian dishes that she had eaten, often more than once – jollof rice, ofada stew, moi moi, egusi soup, onugbu soup, et cetera. What was I to do – create a new dish? I was determined to do so if necessary, but I discovered from sounding her out that there were still some Nigerian dishes that she did not know about. So, I "washed my hands," as we say in Nigeria to describe heartfelt cooking, and prepared coconut rice and assorted meat goulash as well as pounded yam with nsala soup. Everything went very well, and Ella was quite ecstatic. What was it about the proposal then that she seemed to find somehow shameful? Why did she invent a more fanciful story? Was there a lesson there that I had missed or had it all been part of being Ella? Or was I overthinking everything?

What had I missed that was probably always in plain sight? My love for Ella had been as deep as her love for me. When I told a psychiatrist a long time ago that J made my heart joyful, I really didn't know what I was talking about. It was Ella that infused me with indescribable joy, the sort that the desert-weary traveler feels after a mystic rain bath. But Ella and Joel couldn't simply have accidentally fallen into bed together. What I witnessed that night did not seem like a union between fresh lovers. Both of them appeared to already understand each other's bodies and passions. What I witnessed must have been building up or already coursing for some time, even as we paraded ourselves as the best of friends and pledged our lifelong devotion to one another like garrulous waterfalls. The thought was like a knife thrust deeper into my heart.

Poor Sal, she had not foreseen this clearly at all. We had

all come to believe that Sal had "the eye." I had been reluctant to believe such a fairytale – until our road trip that never left the garage. Ella had decided to go to Wyoming to surprise her parents, so I proposed a road trip for four of us. We would drive from Houston through Denver to Wyoming. My cousin, Julia, had told me heady tales about the road trips she had taken with her friends and Uncle Ibe's daughters from Paris to Lisbon, from Paris to Minsk, and from Paris to Madrid.

"You won't believe how much fun it is."

"I don't like driving long distances," I said.

"It's not about the driving. It's about the fellowship, the sights, the experience. You can share the driving with Ella and maybe invite another couple along too. I'm taking an even longer trip, from Paris to Athens, with Chi Girl and Amaka next month. We can't wait."

Chi Girl or Chinenye and Amaka or Nwamaka were Uncle Ibe's children. Julia had helped them move to Paris for graduate studies, and they had decided to stay back in France to work for a while. Uncle Ibe had exhausted all the proverbs that he knew and fashioned many that he never did all in a bid to convince them to return to Nigeria and settle down. They kept assuring him that they would do so eventually. "What goes up must surely come down," he finally told them. Meanwhile, the three of them formed "a tight sisterhood," as Julia described their bond, even though they now lived in different parts of France.

When I told Ella about the idea of a road trip, she was thrilled. Both Joel and Sal were also excited, so we began to work out the details. We would take turns driving and make stops every few hours. Since Ella had the newest and finest car, Joel and Sal would sleep over in our house the night before, and we would set off at dawn with Ella driving the first few hours. We made a list of the things we would most likely need and set a firm date. It was when we confirmed our travel dates that Sal suddenly said

"Someone, some people coming. Trip unlikely." She sometimes spoke her prophecies like a telegram. No preamble, just that announcement. I doubted her. But two people did arrive on the eve of our departure – Ella's parents. They had urgently flown to New York the previous day to see an old friend who was dying in hospital and were on their way back to Wyoming when the plane developed a technical problem and was diverted to Houston. They then decided to surprise us. Ella was flabbergasted because her parents rarely went anywhere. Was it possible that Sal somehow found out about this surprise one week in advance? I asked myself. I had to concede that she indeed had "the eye" and that she probably always had it.

Sal had grown up in a small village in Guadeloupe where her mother made her living as a diviner. Everyone realized early that Sal could see in uncommon ways. She sometimes said things that had not happened and then more often than not they would happen. But she wasn't a diviner, she explained, because she had long periods when she saw nothing. Then, when she least expected it, she would look at something and see more than what she was looking at, either the past or the future. As she grew up, she learned to sometimes keep her visions to herself because some of them were capable of causing conflicts. The day she walked past a woman whom she "saw" planned to poison her husband, she went to her mother and asked that she rid her of her gift. She explained to her that she couldn't. She went to the priest, but he only blessed her and prayed for her. She then went to the police, but she had no evidence, so they told her to beware of committing slander. She summoned the courage to go to the man whose life was in danger, but he labeled her "a troublemaker." She left her village as soon as she could and moved to the city, Basse-Terre, then to Memphis. She hoped that traveling across the ocean would annul her gift of prophecy, but that didn't happen.

The day she walked into a store and saw Joel, she knew she was looking at her husband. But there were dark clouds that she couldn't figure out, so she was afraid that maybe he would one day break her heart. Her gift sometimes yielded incomplete visions, especially about people close to her, so maybe that explained the dark clouds. She didn't see him again for a long time, and she had begun to conclude – with relief – that she had lost the gift when their paths crossed again. After they were married, Sal was determined to dispel those dark clouds. Whatever Joel desired she would provide with utmost devotion. A few years later, when they began planning to have children, she was certain that she had succeeded. Apparently, she did not. What sort of gift was it anyway, I wondered again, to sometimes see clearly into the future of other people but not those whose lives were bound closely to yours? How would someone like Sal, who believed in love and truth with every ounce of her humanity, cope with something like this?

As I stood, transfixed, looking at Ella and Joel that night, my mind combed through our lives in a few jumbled seconds or so, but the more I sought for answers the more my questions ricocheted back to me.

Suddenly, everything began to happen in slow motion. I heard the train whistle begin as if from a distance and then rise to a crescendo. I heard the thundering waves pound in my ears like the horsemen of the apocalypse. And I saw a riot of patterns, more patterns than I had ever seen before, patterns and patterns and still more patterns, begin their cascade right in front of me. I watched myself leave my body. I pushed away Ella's held-out hands as if they were feathers and grabbed her by the throat. She began to scream. I tightened my chokehold, rendering her voiceless. She started flailing as if her body could speak for her instead. I increased the pressure and throttled her to death like a chicken. Joel tried to come to her rescue. I grabbed him as if he was the last item in a burger shop and squeezed him until he fizzed and popped like a soda bottle and his insides began to drip all over the carpet. I dropped him to expire on the floor. But my anger did not abate. I began to tear apart the room. I smashed the CD player, ripped up the mattress, the closet, clothes, mirrors and everything in sight until there was nothing left to destroy. I was in such a tidal rage that I went into the bathroom and ripped up the toilet from the floor and stuck Ella's head into it. I tore out Joel's exposed intestines and stuffed them into his mouth. Still, my anger did not abate. I rushed to the kitchen, grabbed the lighter, gathered together as many combustible items as I could and set the apartment ablaze. Still, my anger did not abate. I grabbed the gun that Ella had bought "to defend herself" when I left for Memphis and went out into the night. I would take a few human heads – no, a lot of human heads – with me to the other world. And when I meet Ella and Joel over there, I would kill them again.

But there was something that held me back. I could feel raindrops on my body, dewy drops from my grandfather's wall, and I returned to myself. Everything had happened so fast that Ella was still holding out her hands and whimpering and Joel was still wriggling into his clothes. But I hardly saw them. In front of me was my grandfather's wall, my wall, and on a corner of it were two new paintings – a number, 44, and another number, 88.

"Please, Ile, please don't kill me," Ella pleaded with a rush of words as if she feared she had only a few more seconds to convince me to spare her life. "Please, don't kill me. I beg you in the name of God..."

I looked at her for a minute or so that seemed like forever.

"It is finished," I said to her as I turned to leave the room.

I could see her eyes grow big as if she was shocked that she was still alive or that I was not going to murder her. She appeared to suddenly remember that she was still naked and began to try to cover herself with her hands.

When I kneeled in front of my grandfather's grave in Stellenbosch, I had whispered to his spirit: "I understand." Then. Now. The fanfare of the seasons. There. Here. The mantra of time-traveling murals. King Lazarus. Umfundisi. Crossroads. Levitations.

What would our lives be without the magic and mystery of being? Regardless. I understood that his life made everything that I witnessed that night ridiculous. My heart was breaking like a glass window assaulted with a boulder and there were tears in my eyes, but I understood even then that my story had become – and had always been – bigger than Ella and Joel. I understood why my grandfather had taken me deeper and deeper into the forest. I understood the sense of arterial newness in that second sentence in the inside back cover of his atlas, his book of everything.

I have seen the future, and it is newer than the past.

———

Stellenbosch, South Africa
October 2, 2017

www.ingramcontent.com/pod-product-compliance
Lightning Source LLC
LaVergne TN
LVHW041937070526
838199LV00051BA/2826